THE PILGRIM'S PROGRESS

by

JOHN BUNYAN

ABRIDGED

A BANCROFT

CLASSIC

BANCROFT BOOKS

LONDON

BANCROFT BOOKS
49–50 Poland Street
London W.1

First published in the "Bancroft Classics"
in 1970
This impression 1972

430 00395 1

THE FIRST PART

From this world
to that which is to come
delivered under the similitude
of a dream
Wherein is discovered
the manner of his setting out
his dangerous journey
and his safe arrival at the
desired countrey

I HAVE USED SIMILITUDES
Hos. 12. 10.

AS I WALKED through the wilderness of this world, I lighted on a certain place, where was a den; and I laid me down in that place to sleep: and as I slept, I dreamed a dream. I dreamed, and, behold I saw a man cloathed with rags, standing in a certain place, with his face from his own house, a book in his hand, and a great burden upon his back. I looked, and saw him open the book, and read therein; and as he read, he wept and trembled; and not being able longer to contain, he brake out with a lamentable cry, saying, What shall I do?

In this plight, therefore, he went home, and refrained himself as long as he could, that his wife and children should not perceive his distress; but he could not be silent long, because that his trouble increased. Wherefore at length he brake his mind to his wife and children; and thus he began to talk to them: O my dear wife, said he, and you, the children of my bowels, I, your dear friend, am in myself undone, by reason of a burden that lieth hard upon me; moreover, I am for certain informed that this our city will be burned with fire from heaven; in which fearful overthrow, both myself, with thee, my wife, and you, my sweet babes, shall miserably come to ruin, except (the which yet I see not) some way of escape can be found, whereby we may be delivered. At this, his relations were sore amazed; not for that they believed that what he had said to them was true, but because they thought that some frenzy distemper had got into his head; therefore, it drawing towards night, and they hoping that sleep might settle his brains, with all haste they got him to bed. But the night was as troublesome to him as the day; wherefore instead of sleeping, he spent it in sighs and tears. So when the morning was come, they would know how he did; he told them, worse and worse; he also set to talking to them again, but they began to be hardened. They also thought to drive away his distemper by harsh and surly carriages to him. Sometimes they would deride, sometimes they would chide, and sometimes they would quite neglect him. Wherefore he began to retire himself to his chamber to pray for, and pity them, and also to condole his own misery. He would also walk solitarily in the fields, sometimes reading, and sometimes praying; and thus for some days he spent his time.

Now I saw upon a time, when he was walking in the fields, that he was, as he was wont, reading in his book, and greatly distressed in his mind; and as he read, he burst out, as he had done before, crying, What shall I do to be saved?

I saw also that he looked this way and that way, as if he would run; yet he stood still, because, as I perceived, he could not tell which way to go. I looked then, and saw a man named Evangelist coming to him, who asked, Wherefore dost thou cry?

He answered, Sir, I perceive, by the book in my hand, that I am condemned to die, and after that to come to judgment; and I find that I am not willing to do the first, nor able to do the second.

Then said Evangelist, Why not willing to die, since this life is attended with so many evils? The man answered, Because I fear that this burden that is upon my back will sink me lower than the grave; and I shall fall into Tophet. And, Sir, if I be not fit to go to prison, I am not fit, I am sure, to go to judgment, and from thence to execution; and the thoughts of these things make me cry.

Then said Evangelist, If this be thy condition, why standest thou still? He answered, Because I know not whither to go. Then he gave him a parchment roll, and there was written within, Fly from the wrath to come.

The man, therefore, read it, and looking upon Evangelist very carefully, said, Whither must I fly? Then said Evangelist, pointing with his finger over a very wide field, Do you see yonder wicket-gate? The man said, No. Then said the other, Do you see yonder shining light? He said, I think I do. Then said Evangelist, Keep that light in your eye, and go up directly thereto, so shalt thou see the gate; at which, when thou knockest, it shall be told thee what thou shalt do.

So I saw in my dream that the man began to run. Now, he had not run far from his own door, but his wife and children perceiving it, began to cry after him to return; but the man put his fingers in his ears, and ran on, crying, Life! life! Eternal life! So he looked not behind him, but fled towards the middle of the plain.

The neighbours also came out to see him run, and as he ran, some mocked, others threatened, and some cried after him to return; and among those that did so, there were two that were resolved to fetch him back by force. The name of the one was Obstinate, and the name of the other Pliable. Now by this time, the man was got a good distance from them; but, however, they were resolved to pursue him; which they did, and in a little time the overtook him. Then said the man, Neighboours, wherefore are ye come? They said, To persuade you to go back with us. But he said, That can by no means be. You dwell, said he, in the City of Destruction, the place also where I was born; I see it to be so; and dying there, sooner or later, you will sink lower than the grave, into a place that burns with fire and brimstone. Be content, good neighbours, and go along with me.

OBSTINATE. What, said Obstinate, and leave our friends and our comforts behind us?

CHRISTIAN. Yes, said Christian, for that was his name, because that all which you shall forsake is not worthy to be compared with a little of that which I am seeking to enjoy; and if you will go along with me, and hold it, you shall fare as I myself, for there, where I go, is enough and to spare. Come away, and prove my words.

OBSTINATE. What are the things you seek, since you leave all the world to find them?

CHRISTIAN. I seek an inheritance incorruptible, undefiled, and that fadeth not away, and it is laid up in heaven, and safe there, to be bestowed, at the time appointed, on them that diligently seek it. Read it so, if you will, in my book.

OBSTINATE. Tush, said Obstinate, away with your book; will you go back with us, or no?

CHRISTIAN. No, not I, saith the other; because I have laid my hand to the plow.

OBSTINATE. Come, then, neighbour Pliable, let us turn again, and go home without him; there is a company of these crazed-headed coxcombs, that when they take a fancy by the end, are wiser in their own eyes than seven men that can render a reason.

PLIABLE. Then said Pliable, Do not revile; if what the good Christian says is true, the things he looks after are better than ours; my heart inclines to go with my neighbour.

OBSTINATE. What! more fools still? Be ruled by me, and go back; who knows whither such a brain-sick fellow will lead you? Go back, go back, and be wise.

CHRISTIAN. Nay, but do thou come with thy neighbour Pliable: there are such things to be had which I spoke of, and many more glories besides; if you believe not me, read here in this book, and for the truth of what is expressed therein, behold, all is confirmed by the blood of him that made it.

PLIABLE. Well, neighbour Obstinate, saith Pliable. I begin to come to a point; I intend to go along with this good man, and to cast in my lot with him. But, my good companion, do you know the way to this desired place?

CHRISTIAN. I am directed by a man whose name is Evangelist, to speed me to a little gate that is before us, where we shall receive instructions about the way.

PLIABLE. Come then, good neighbour, let us be going. Then they went both together.

OBSTINATE. And I will go to my place, said Obstinate; I will be no companion of such mis-led fantastical fellows.

Now I saw in my dream, that when Obstinate was gone back, Christian and Pliable went talking over the plain; and thus they began their discourse.

CHRISTIAN. Come, neighbour Pliable, how do you do? I am glad you are persuaded to go along with me; had even Obstinate himself but felt what I have felt, of the powers and terrors of what is yet unseen, he would not thus lightly have given us the back.

PLIABLE. Come, neighbour Christian, since there is none but us two here, tell me now further, what the things are, and how to be enjoyed, whither we are going.

CHRISTIAN. I can better conceive of them with my mind, than speak of them with my tongue; but yet since you are desirous to know, I will read of them in my book.

PLIABLE. And do you think that the words of your book are certainly true?

CHRISTIAN. Yes, verily, for it was made by him that cannot lie.

PLIABLE. Well said. What things are they?

CHRISTIAN. There is an endless kingdom to be inhabited, and everlasting life to be given us, that we may inhabit that kingdom for ever.

PLIABLE. Well said. And what else?

CHRISTIAN. There are crowns of glory to be given us, and garments that will make us shine like the sun in the firmament of heaven!

PLIABLE. This is very pleasant. And what else?

CHRISTIAN. There shall be no more crying, nor sorrow; for he that is owner of the place will wipe all tears from our eyes.

PLIABLE. And what company shall we have there?

CHRISTIAN. There we shall be with seraphims, and cherubims, creatures that will dazzle your eyes to look on them. There, also, you shall meet with thousands and ten thousands that have gone before us to that place; none of them are hurtful, but loving and holy, every one walking in the sight of God, and standing in his presence with acceptance for ever; in a word, there we shall see the elders with their golden crowns; there we shall see the holy virgins with their golden harps; there we shall see men, that by the world were cut in pieces, burnt in flames, eaten of beasts, drowned in the seas, for the love that they bare to the Lord of the place; all well, and clothed with immortality as with a garment.

PLIABLE. The hearing of this is enough to ravish one's heart; but are these things to be enjoyed? How shall we get to be sharers thereof?

CHRISTIAN. The Lord, the governor of the country, hath recorded that in this book, the substance of which is, if we be truly willing to have it, he will bestow it upon us freely.

PLIABLE. Well, my good companion, glad am I to hear of these things; come on, let us mend our pace.

CHRISTIAN. I cannot go so fast as I would, by reason of this burden that is on my back.

Now I saw in my dreams, that, just as they had ended this talk, they drew near to a very miry slough that was in the midst of the plain; and they, being heedless, did both fall suddenly into the bog. The name of the slough was Dispond. Here, therefore, they wallowed for a time, being grievously bedaubed with the dirt; and Christian, because of the burden that was on his back, began to sink in the mire.

PLIABLE. Then said Pliable, Ah! neighbour Christian, where are you now?

CHRISTIAN. Truly, said Christian, I do not know.

PLIABLE. At that Pliable began to be offended, and angrily said to his fellow, Is this the happiness you have told me all this while of? If we have such ill speed at our first setting out, what may we expect betwixt this and our journey's end? May I get out again with my life, you shall possess the brave country alone for me. And with that he gave a desperate struggle or two, and got out of the mire on that side of the slough which was next to his own house: so away he went, and Christian saw him no more.

Wherefore Christian was left to tumble in the Slough of Dispond alone; but still he endeavoured to struggle to that side of the slough that was still further from his own house, and next to the wicket-gate; the which he did, but could not get out, because of the burden that was upon his back. But I beheld in my dream, that a man came to him, whose name was Help, and asked him what he did there?

CHRISTIAN. Sir, said, Christian, I was bid go this way by a man called Evangelist, who directed me also to yonder gate, that I might escape the wrath to come. And as I was going thither, I fell in here.

HELP. But why did you not look for the steps?

CHRISTIAN. Fear followed me so hard, that I fled the next way, and fell in.

HELP. Then said he, Give me thy hand; so he gave him his hand, and he drew him out, and set him upon sound ground, and bid him go on his way.

Then I stepped to him that plucked him out, and said, Sir, wherefore (since over this place is the way from the City of Destruction, to yonder gate) is it that this plat is not mended, that poor travellers might go thither with more security? And he said unto me, This miry slough is such a place as cannot be mended. It is the descent whither the scum and filth that attends conviction for sin, doth continually run, and therefore it is called the Slough of Dispond; for still, as the sinner is awakened about his lost condition, there ariseth in his soul many fears, and doubts, and discouraging apprehensions, which all of them get together, and settle in this place. And this is the reason of the badness of this ground.

Now as Christian was walking solitarily by himself, he espied one afar off come crossing over the field to meet him; and their hap was to meet just as they were crossing the way of each other. The gentleman's name that met him was Mr. Worldly Wiseman; he dwelt in the town of Carnal Policy, a very great town, and also hard by from whence Christian came. This man, then, meeting with Christian, and having some inkling of him, for Christian's setting forth from the City of Destruction was much noised abroad, began thus to enter into some talk with Christian.

WORLDLY WISEMAN. How now, good fellow, whither away after this burdened manner?

CHRISTIAN. A burdened manner, indeed, as ever, I think, poor creature had! And whereas you ask me, Whither away? I tell you, Sir, I am going to yonder wicket-gate before me; for there, as I am informed, I shall be put into a way to be rid of my heavy burden.

WORLDLY WISEMAN. Hast thou a wife and children?

CHRISTIAN. Yes; but I am so laden with this burden, that I cannot take that pleasure in them as formerly; methinks I am as if I had none.

WORLDLY WISEMAN. Wilt thou hearken unto me if I give thee counsel?

CHRISTIAN. If it be good, I will; for I stand in need of good counsel.

WORLDLY WISEMAN. I would advise thee, then, that thou with all speed get thyself rid of thy burden; for thou wilt never be settled in thy mind till then; nor canst thou enjoy the benefits of the blessing which God hath bestowed upon thee till then.

CHRISTIAN. That is that which I seek for, even to be rid of this heavy burden; but get it off myself, I cannot; nor is there any man in our country that can take it off my shoulders; therefore am I going this way, as I told you, that I may be rid of my burden.

WORLDLY WISEMAN. Who bid thee go this way to be rid of thy burden?

CHRISTIAN. A man that appeared to me to be a very great and honourable person; his name, as I remember, is Evangelist.

WORLDLY WISEMAN. I beshrew him for his counsel! there is not a more dangerous and troublesome way in the world than is that unto which he hath directed thee; and that thou shalt find, if thou wilt be ruled by his counsel. Thou hast met with something, as I perceive already; for I see the dirt of the Slough of Dispond is upon thee; but that slough is the beginning of the sorrows that do attend those that go on in that way. Hear me, I am older than thou; thou art like to meet with, on the way which thou goest, wearisomeness, painfulness, hunger, perils, nakedness, sword, lions, dragons, darkness, and, in a word, death, and what not! These things are certainly true, having been confirmed by many testimonies. And why should a man so carelessly cast away himself, by giving heed to a stranger?

CHRISTIAN. Why, Sir, this burden upon my back is more terrible to me than are all these things which you have mentioned; nay, methinks I care not what I meet with in the way, if so be I can also meet with deliverance from my burden.

WORLDLY WISEMAN. How camest thou by the burden at first.

CHRISTIAN. By reading this book in my hand.

WORLDLY WISEMAN. I thought so; and it is happened unto thee as to other weak men, who, meddling with things too high for them, do suddenly fall into thy distractions; which distractions do not only unman men, as thine, I perceive, have done thee, but they run them upon desperate ventures, to obtain they know not what.

10

CHRISTIAN. I know what I would obtain; it is ease for my heavy burden.

WORLDLY WISEMAN. But why wilt thou seek for ease this way, seeing so many dangers attend it? especially since, hadst thou but patience to hear me, I could direct thee to the obtaining of what thou desirest, without the dangers that thou in this way wilt run thyself into; yea, and the remedy is at hand. Besides, I will add, that, instead of those dangers, thou shalt meet with much safety, friendship, and content.

CHRISTIAN. Pray, open this secret to me.

WORLDLY WISEMAN. Why, in yonder village—the village is named Morality—there dwells a gentleman whose name is Legality, a very judicious man, and a man of a very good name, that has skill to help men off with such burdens as thine are from their shoulders: yea, to my knowledge, he hath done a great deal of good this way; aye, and besides, he hath skill to cure those that are somewhat crazed in their wits with their burdens. To him, as I said, thou mayest go, and be helped presently. His house is not quite a mile from this place, and if he should not be at home himself, he hath a pretty young man to his son, whose name is Civility, that can do it (to speak on) as well the old gentleman himself; there, I say, thou mayest be eased of thy burden; and if thou art not minded to go back to thy former habitation, as, indeed, I would not wish, thou mayest send for thy wife and children to thee to this village, where there are houses now stand empty, one of which thou mayest have at reasonable rates; provision is there also cheap and good; and that which will make thy life the more happy is, to be sure, there thou shalt live by honest neighbours, in credit and good fashion.

Now was Christian somewhat at a stand; but presently he concluded, If this be true, which this gentleman hath said, my wisest course is to take his advice; and with that he thus further spoke.

CHRISTIAN. Sir, which is my way to this honest man's house?

WORLDLY WISEMAN. Do you see yonder hill?

CHRISTIAN. Yes, very well.

WORLDLY WISEMAN. By that hill you must go, and the first house you come at is his.

So Christian turned out of his way, to go to Mr. Legality's house for help; but, behold, when he was got now hard by the hill, it seemed so high, and also that side of it that was next the wayside, did hang so much over, that Christian was afraid to venture further, lest the hill should fall on his head; wherefore there he stood still, and wotted not what to do. Also his burden now seemed heavier to him, than while he was in his way. There came also flashes of fire out of the hill, that made Christian afraid that he should be burned. Here, therefore, he sweat and did quake for fear. And now he began to be sorry that he had taken Mr. Worldly Wiseman's counsel. And with that he saw Evangelist coming to meet him; at the sight also of whom he began to blush for shame. So Evangelist drew nearer and nearer; and coming up to him, he looked upon him with a severe and dreadful countenance, and thus began to reason with Christian.

11

EVANGELIST. What dost thou here, Christian? said he: at which words Christian knew not what to answer; wherefore at present he stood speechless before him. Then said Evangelist further, Art not thou the man that I found crying without the walls of the City of Destruction?

CHRISTIAN. Yes, dear Sir, I am the man.

EVANGELIST. Did not I direct thee the way to the little wicket-gate?

CHRISTIAN. Yes, dear Sir, said Christian.

EVANGELIST. How is it, then, that thou art so quickly turned aside? for thou art now out of the way.

CHRISTIAN. I met with a gentleman so soon as I had got over the Slough of Dispond, who persuaded me that I might, in the village before me, find a man that could take off my burden.

EVANGELIST. What was he?

CHRISTIAN. He looked like a gentleman, and talked much to me, and got me at last to yield; so I came hither: but when I beheld this hill, and how it hangs over the way, I suddenly made a stand, lest it should fall on my head.

EVANGELIST. What said that gentleman to you?

CHRISTIAN. Why, he asked me whither I was going? And I told him.

EVANGELIST. And what said he then?

CHRISTIAN. He asked me if I had a family? And I told him. But, said I, I am so laden with the burden that is on my back, that I cannot take pleasure in them as formerly.

EVANGELIST. And what said he then?

CHRISTIAN. He bid me with speed get rid of my burden; and I told him it was ease that I sought. And, said I, I am therefore going to yonder gate, to receive further direction how I may get to the place of deliverance. So he said that he would show me a better way, and short, not so attended with difficulties as the way, Sir, that you set me in; which way, said he, will direct you to a gentleman's house that hath skill to take off these burdens: so I believed him, and turned out of that way into this, if haply I might be soon eased of my burden. But when I came to this place, and beheld things as they are, I stopped for fear (as I said) of danger: but I now know not what to do.

EVANGELIST. Then, said Evangelist, stand still a little, that I may show thee the words of God. So he stood trembling. Then said Evangelist, See that ye refuse not him that speaketh. For if they escaped not who refused him that spake on earth, much more shall not we escape, if we turn away from him that speaketh from heaven. He said, moreover, Now the just shall live by faith: but if any man draw back, my soul shall shall have no pleasure in him. He also did thus apply them: Thou art the man that art running into this misery; thou hast begun to reject the counsel of the Most High, and to draw back thy foot from the way of peace, even almost to the hazarding of thy perdition.

Then Christian fell down at his foot as dead, crying, Woe is me, for I am undone! At the sight of which Evangelist caught him by the right hand, saying, All manner of sin and blasphemies shall be forgiven unto men; be not faithless, but believing. Then did Christian again a little revive, and stood up trembling, as at first, before Evangelist.

Then Evangelist proceeded, saying, Give more earnest heed to the things that I shall tell thee of. I will now show thee who it was that deluded thee, and who it was also to whom he sent thee.—The man that met thee is one Worldly Wiseman, and rightly is he so called; partly, because he savoureth only the doctrine of this world (therefore he always goes to the town of Morality to church); and partly because he loveth that doctrine best, for it saveth him best from the cross. And because he is of this carnal temper, therefore he seeketh to prevent my ways, though right. Now there are three things in this man's counsel, that thou must utterly abhor.

1. His turning thee out of the way.

2. His labouring to render the cross odious to thee.

And, 3. His setting thy feet in that way that leadeth unto the administration of death.

First, Thou must abhor his turning thee out of the way; yea, and thine own consenting thereto: because this is to reject the counsel of God for the sake of the counsel of a Worldly Wiseman. The Lord says, Strive to enter in at the strait gate, the gate to which I send thee; for strait is the gate which leadeth unto life, and few there be that find it. From this little wicket-gate, and from the way thereto, hath this wicked man turned thee, to the bringing of thee almost to destruction; hate, therefore, his turning thee out of the way, and abhor thyself for hearkening to him.

Secondly, Thou must abhor his labouring to render the cross odious unto thee; for thou art to prefer it before the treasures in Egypt. Besides, the King of glory hath told thee, that he that will save his life shall lose it. And he that comes after him, and hates not his father, and mother, and wife, and children, and brethren, and sisters, yea, and his own life also, he cannot be my disciple. I say, therefore, for man to labour to persuade thee, that that shall by thy death, without which, the Truth hath said, thou canst not have eternal life; this doctrine thou must abhor.

Thirdly, Thou must hate his setting of thy feet in the way that leadeth to the ministration of death. And for this thou must consider to whom he sent thee, and also how unable that person was to deliver thee from thy burden.

He to whom thou wast sent for ease, being by name Legality, is the son of the bond-woman which now is, and is in bondage with her children; and is, in a mystery, this Mount Sinai, which thou hast feared will fall on thy head. Now, if she, with her children, are in bondage, how canst thou expect by them to be made free? This Legality, therefore, is not able to set thee free from thy burden. No man was as yet ever rid of his burden by him; no, nor ever is like to be: ye cannot be justified by the works of the law: for by the deeds of the law no man living can be rid of his burden: therefore, Mr. Worldly Wiseman is an alien, and Mr. Legality is a cheat; and for his son Civility, notwithstanding his simpering looks, he is but a hypocrite, and cannot help thee. Believe me, there is nothing in all this noise, that thou hast heard of these sottish men, but a design to beguile thee of thy salvation, by turning thee from the way in which I had set thee. After this Evangelist called aloud to the heavens for confirmation of what he had said: and with that there came words and fire out of the mountain under which poor Christian stood, that made the hair of his flesh stand up. The words were thus pronounced: As many as are of the works of the law are under the curse; for it is written, Cursed is every one that continueth not in all things which are written in the book of the law to do them.

Now Christian looked for nothing but death, and began to cry out lamentably; even cursing the time in which he met with Mr. Worldly Wiseman; still calling himself a thousand fools for hearkening to his counsel; he also was greatly ashamed to think that this gentleman's arguments, flowing only from the flesh, should have the prevalency with him as to cause him to forsake the right way. This done, he applied himself again to Evangelist, in words and sense as follows:

CHRISTIAN. Sir, what think you? Is there hope? May I now go back, and go up to the wicket-gate? Shall I not be abandoned for this, and sent back from thence ashamed? I am sorry I have hearkened to this man's counsel. But may my sin be forgiven?

EVANGELIST. Then said Evangelist to him, Thy sin is very great, for by it thou hast committed two evils; thou hast forsaken the way that is good, to tread in forbidden paths; yet will the man at the gate receive thee, for he has goodwill for men; only, said he, take heed that thou turn not aside again, lest thou perish from the way, when his wrath is kindled but a little. Then did Christian address himself to go back; and Evangelist, after he had kissed him, gave him one smile, and bid him God-speed. So he went on with haste, neither spake he to any man by the way; nor, if any asked him, would he vouchsafe them an answer. He went like one that was all the while treading on forbidden ground, and could by no means think himself safe, till again he was got into the way which he left, to follow Mr. Worldly Wiseman's counsel. So, in process of time, Christian got up to the gate. Now, over the gate there was written, Knock, and it shall be opened unto you.

He knocked, therefore, more than once or twice, saying:

> May I now enter here? Will he within
> Open to sorry me, though I have been
> An undeserving rebel? Then shall I
> Not fail to sing his lasting praise on high.

At last there came a grave person to the gate, named Good-will, who asked who was there? and whence he came? and what he would have?

CHRISTIAN. Here is a poor burdened sinner. I come from the City of Destruction, but am going to Mount Zion, that I may be delivered from the wrath to come. I would, therefore, Sir, since I am informed that by this gate is the way thither, know if you are willing to let me in?

14

GOOD-WILL. I am willing with all my heart, said he; and with that he opened the gate.

So when Christian was stepping in, the other gave him a pull. Then said Christian, What means that? The other told him, A little distance from this gate, there is erected a strong castle, of which Beelzebub is the captain; from thence, both he and they that are with him shoot arrows at those that come up to this gate, if haply they may die before they can enter in.

Then said Christian, I rejoice and tremble. So when he was got in, the man of the gate asked him who directed him thither?

CHRISTIAN. Evangelist bid me come hither, and knock (as I did); and he said that you, Sir, would tell me what I must do.

GOOD-WILL. An open door is set before thee, and no man can shut it.

CHRISTIAN. Now I begin to reap the benefits of my hazards.

GOOD-WILL. But how is it that you came alone?

CHRISTIAN. Because none of my neighbours saw their danger, as I saw mine.

GOOD-WILL. Did any of them know of your coming?

CHRISTIAN. Yes; my wife and children saw me at the first, and called after me to turn again; also, some of my neighbours stood crying and calling after me to return; but I put my fingers in my ears, and so came on my way.

GOOD-WILL. But did none of them follow you, to persuade you to go back?

CHRISTIAN. Yes, both Obstinate and Pliable; but when they saw that they could not prevail, Obstinate went railing back, but Pliable came with me a little way.

GOOD-WILL. But why did he not come through?

CHRISTIAN. We, indeed, came both together, until we came at the Slough of Dispond, into the which we also suddenly fell. And then was my neighbour, Pliable, discouraged, and would not adventure further. Wherefore, getting out again on that side next to his own house, he told me that I should possess the brave country alone for him; so he went his way, and I came mine—he after Obstinate, and I to his gate.

GOOD-WILL. Then said Good-will, Alas, poor man! is the celestial glory of so small esteem with him, that he counteth it not worth running the hazards of a few difficulties to obtain it?

CHRISTIAN. Truly, said Christian, I have said the truth of Pliable, and if I should also say all the truth of myself, it will appear there is no betterment betwixt him and myself. It is true, he went back to his own house, but I also turned aside to go in the way of death, being persuaded thereto by the carnal arguments of one Mr. Worldly Wiseman.

GOOD-WILL. Oh! did he light upon you? What! he would have had you a sought for ease at the hands of Mr. Legality. They are, both of them, a very cheat. But did you take his counsel?

CHRISTIAN. Yes, as far as I durst; I went to find out Mr. Legality, until I thought that the mountain that stands by his house would have fallen upon my head; wherefore, there I was forced to stop.

15

GOOD-WILL. That mountain has been the death of many, and will be the death of many more; it is well you escaped being by it dashed in pieces.

CHRISTIAN. Why, truly, I do not know what had become of me there, had not Evangelist happily met me again, as I was musing in the midst of my dumps; but it was God's mercy that he came to me again, for else I had never come hither. But now I am come, such a one as I am, more fit, indeed, for death, by that mountain, than thus to stand talking with my Lord; but O! what a favour is this to me, that yet I am admitted entrance here!

GOOD-WILL. We make no objections against any, notwithstanding all that they have done before they come hither. They are in no wise cast out; and therefore, good Christian, come a little way with me, and I will teach thee about the way thou must go. Look before thee; dost thou see this narrow way? That is the way thou must go; it was cast up by the patriarchs, prophets, Christ, and his apostles; and it is as straight as a rule can make it. This is the way thou must go.

CHRISTIAN. But, said Christian, are there no turnings nor windings, by which a stranger may lose his way?

GOOD-WILL. Yes, there are many ways butt down upon this, and they are crooked and wide. But thus thou mayest distinguish the right from the wrong, the right only being straight and narrow.

Then I saw in my dream, that Christian asked him further if he could not help him off with his burden that was upon his back; for as yet he had not got rid thereof, nor could he by any means get it off without help.

He told him, As to thy burden, be content to bear it, until thou comest to the place of deliverance; for there it will fall from thy back of itself.

Then Christian began to gird up his loins, and to address himself to his journey. So the other told him, That by that he was gone some distance from the gate, he would come at the house of the Interpreter; at whose door he should knock, and he would show him excellent things. Then Christian took his leave of his friend, and he again bid him God-speed.

Then he went on till he came at the house of the Interpreter, where he knocked; at last one came to the door, and asked who was there.

CHRISTIAN. Sir, said Christian, I am a man that am come from the City of Destruction, and am going to the Mount Zion; and I was told by the man that stands at the gate, at the head of this way, that if I called here, you would show me excellent things, such as would be a help to me in my journey.

INTERPRETER. Then said the Interpreter, Come in; I will show thee that which will be profitable to thee. So he commanded his man to light the candle, and bid Christian follow him: so he had him into a private room, and bid his man open a door; the which when he had done, Christian saw the picture of a very grave person hang up against the wall; and this was the fashion of it. It had eyes lifted up to heaven, the best of books in his hand, the law of truth was written upon his lips, the world was behind his back. It stood as if it pleaded with men, and a crown of gold did hang over its head.

CHRISTIAN. Then said Christian, What meaneth this?

INTERPRETER. Whereas thou seest him with his eyes lift up to heaven, the best of books in his hand, and the law of truth writ on his lips, it is to show thee, that his work is to know and unfold dark things to sinners; even as also thou seest him stand as if he pleaded with men; and whereas thou seest the world as cast behind him, and that a crown hangs over his head, that is to show thee that slighting and despising the things that are present, for the love that he hath to his Master's service, he is sure in the world that comes next to have glory for his reward. Now, said the Interpreter, I have showed thee this picture first, because the man whose picture this is, is the only man whom the Lord of the place whither thou art going, hath authorized to be thy guide in all difficult places thou mayest meet with in the way; wherefore, take good heed to what I have showed thee, and bear well in thy mind what thou hast seen, lest in thy journey thou meet with some that pretend to lead thee right, but their way goes down to death.

Then he took him by the hand, and led him into a very large parlour that was full of dust, because never swept; the which, after he had reviewed a little while, the Interpreter called for a man to sweep. Now, when he began to sweep, the dust began so abundantly to fly about, that Christian had almost therewith been choked. Then said the Interpreter to a damsel that stood by, Bring hither the water, and sprinkle the room; the which, when she had done, it was swept and cleansed with pleasure.

CHRISTIAN. Then said Christian, What means this?

INTERPRETER. The Interpreter answered, This parlour is the heart of a man that was never sanctified by the sweet grace of the gospel; the dust is his original sin and inward corruptions, that have defiled the whole man. He that began to sweep at first, is the Law; but she that brought water, and did sprinkle it, is the Gospel. Now, whereas thou sawest, that so soon as the first began to sweep, the dust did so fly about that the room by him could not be cleansed, but that thou wast almost choked therewith; this is to show thee, that the law, instead of cleansing the heart (by its working) from sin, doth revive, put strength into, and increase it in the soul, even as it doth discover and forbid it, for it doth not give power to subdue.

Again, as thou sawest the damsel sprinkle the room with water, upon which it was cleansed with pleasure; this is to show thee, that when the gospel comes in the sweet and precious influences thereof to the heart, then, I say, even as thou sawest the damsel lay the dust by sprinkling the floor with water, so is sin vanquished and subdued, and the soul made clean, through the faith of it, and consequently fit for the King of glory to inhabit.

I saw, moreover, in my dream, that the Interpreter took him by the hand, and had him into a little room, where sat two little children, each one in his chair. The name of the eldest was Passion, and the name of the other Patience. Passion seemed to be much discontented; but Patience was very quiet. Then Christian asked, What is the reason of the discontent of Passion? The Interpreter answered, The Governor of them would have him stay for his best things till the beginning of the next year; but he will have all now; but Patience is willing to wait.

Then I saw that one came to Passion, and brought him a bag of treasure, and poured it down at his feet, the which he took up and rejoiced therein, and withal laughed Patience to scorn. But I beheld but a while, and he had lavished all away, and had nothing left him but rags.

CHRISTIAN. Then said Christian to the Interpreter, Expound this matter more fully to me.

INTERPRETER. So he said, These two lads are figures: Passion, of the men of this world; and Patience, of the men of that which is to come; for, as here thou seest, Passion will have all now this year, that is to say, in this world; so are the men of this world: they must have all their good things now, they cannot stay till next year, that is, until the next world, for their portion of good. That proverb, A bird in the hand is worth two in the bush, is of more authority with them than are all the Divine testimonies of the good of the world to come. But as thou sawest that he had quickly lavished all away, and had presently left him nothing but rags; so will it be with all such men at the end of this world.

CHRISTIAN. Then said Christian, Now I see that Patience has the best wisdom, and that upon many accounts. First, Because he stays for the best things. Second, And also because he will have the glory of his, when the other has nothing but rags.

INTERPRETER. Nay, you may add another, to wit, the glory of the next world will never wear out; but these are suddenly gone. Therefore Passion had not so much reason to laugh at Patience, because he had his good things first, as Patience will have to laugh at Passion, because he had his best things last; for first must give place to last, because last must have his time to come; but last gives place to nothing; for there is not another to succeed. He, therefore, that hath his portion first, must needs have a time to spend it; but he that hath his portion last, must have it lastingly; therefore it is said of Dives, Thou in thy lifetime receivedst thy good things, and likewise Lazarus evil things; but now he is comforted, and thou art tormented.

CHRISTIAN. Then I perceive it is not best to covet things that are now, but to wait for things to come.

INTERPRETER. You say the truth: For the things which are seen are temporal; but the things which are not seen are eternal. But though this be so, yet since things present, and our fleshy appetite, are such near neighbours one to another; and again, because things to come, and carnal sense, are such strangers one to another; therefore it is that the first of these so suddenly fall into amity, and that distance is so continued between the second.

Then I saw in my dream that the Interpreter took Christian by the hand, and led him into a place where was a fire burning against a wall, and one standing by it, always casting much water upon it, to quench it; yet did the fire burn higher and hotter.

Then said Christian, What means this?

The Interpreter answered, This fire is the work of grace that is wrought in the heart; he that casts water upon it, to extinguish and put it out, is the Devil; but in that thou seest the fire notwithstanding burn higher and hotter, thou shalt also see the reason of that. So he had him about to the back side of the wall, where he saw a man with a vessel of oil in his hand, of the which he did also continually cast, but secretly, into the fire.

Then said Christian, What means this?

The Interpreter answered, This is Christ, who continually, with the oil of his grace, maintains the work already begun in the heart: by the means of which, notwithstanding what the devil can do, the souls of his people prove gracious still. And in that thou sawest that the man stood behind the wall to maintain the fire, that is to teach thee that it is hard for the tempted to see how this work of grace is maintained in the soul.

I saw also, that the Interpreter took him again by the hand, and led him into a pleasant place, where was builded a stately palace, beautiful to behold; at the sight of which Christian was greatly delighted; he saw also, upon the top thereof, certain persons walking, who were clothed all in gold.

Then said Christian, May we go in thither?

Then the Interpreter took him, and led him up towards the door of the palace; and behold, at the door stood a great company of men, as desirous to go in, but durst not. There also sat a man at a little distance from the door, at a table-side, with a book and his inkhorn before him, to take the name of him that should enter therein; he saw also, that in the doorway stood many men in armour to keep it, being resolved to do the men that would enter what hurt and mischief they could. Now was Christian somewhat in a maze. At last, when every man started back for fear of the armed men, Christian saw a man of a very stout countenance come up to the man that sat there to write, saying, Set down my name, Sir: the which when he had done, he saw the man draw his sword, and put an helmet upon his head, and rush toward the door upon the armed men, who laid upon him with deadly force: but the man, not at all discouraged, fell to cutting and hacking most fiercely. So after he had received and given many wounds to those that attempted to keep him out, he cut his way through them all, and pressed forward into the palace, at which there was a pleasant voice heard from those that were within, even of those that walked upon the top of the palace, saying:

> Come in, come in;
> Eternal glory thou shalt win.

So he went in, and was clothed with such garments as they. Then Christian smiled and said, I think verily I know the meaning of this.

Now, said Christian, let me go hence. Nay, stay, said the Interpreter, till I have showed thee a little more, and after that thou shalt go on thy way. So he took him by the hand again, and led him into a very dark room, where there sat a man in an iron cage.

Now the man, to look on, seemed very sad; he sat with his eyes looking down to the ground, his hands folded together, and he sighed as if he would break his heart. Then said Christian, What means this? At which the Interpreter bid him talk with the man.

Then said Christian to the man, What art thou? The man answered, I am what I was not once.

CHRISTIAN. What wast thou once?

MAN. The man said, I was once a fair and flourishing professor, both in mine own eyes, and also in the eyes of others; I once was, as I thought, fair for the Celestial City, and had then even joy at the thoughts that I should get thither.

CHRISTIAN. Well, but what art thou now?

MAN. I am now a man of despair, and am shut up in it, as in this iron cage. I cannot get out. O now I cannot!

CHRISTIAN. But how camest thou in this condition?

MAN. I left off to watch and be sober; I laid the reins upon the neck of my lusts; I sinned against the light of the Word, and the goodness of God; I have grieved the Spirit, and he is gone; I tempted the devil, and he is come to me; I have provoked God to anger, and he has left me; I have so hardened my heart, that I cannot repent.

Then said Christian to the Interpreter, But is there no hope for such a man as this? Ask him, said the Interpreter. Nay, said Christian, pray Sir, do you.

INTERPRETER. Then said the Interpreter, Is there no hope, but you must be kept in the iron cage of despair?

MAN. No, none at all.

INTERPRETER. Why, the Son of the Blessed is very pitiful.

MAN. I have crucified him to myself afresh; I have despised his person; I have despised his righteousness; I have counted his blood an unholy thing; I have done despite to the Spirit of grace. Therefore I have shut myself out of all the promises, and there now remains to me nothing but threatenings, dreadful threatenings, fearful threatenings, of certain judgment and fiery indignation, which shall devour me as an adversary.

INTERPRETER. For what did you bring yourself into this condition?

MAN. For the lusts, pleasures, and profits of this world; in the enjoyment of which I did then promise myself much delight; but now every one of those things also bite me, and gnaw me like a burning worm.

INTERPRETER. But canst thou not now repent and turn?

MAN. God hath denied me repentance. His Word gives me no encouragement to believe; yea, himself hath shut me up in this iron cage; nor can all the men in the world let me out. O eternity! eternity! how shall I grapple with the misery that I must meet with in eternity.

INTERPRETER. Then said the Interpreter to Christian, Let this man's misery be remembered by thee, and be an everlasting caution to thee.

CHRISTIAN. Well, said Christian, this is fearful! God help me to watch and be sober, and to pray that I may shun the cause of this man's misery! Sir, is it not time for me to go on my way now?

INTERPRETER. Tarry till I shall show thee one thing more, and then thou shalt go on thy way.

So he took Christian by the hand again, and led him into a chamber, where there was one rising out of bed; and as he put on his raiment, he shook and trembled. Then said Christian, Why doth this man thus tremble? The Interpreter then bid him tell to Christian the reason of his so doing. So he began and said, This night, as I was in my sleep, I dreamed, and behold the heavens grew exceeding black; also it thundered and lightened in most fearful wise, that it put me into an agony; so I looked up in my dream, and saw the clouds rack at an unusual rate, upon which I heard a great sound of a trumpet, and saw also a man sit upon a cloud, attended with the thousands of heaven; they were all in flaming fire: also the heavens were in a burning flame. I heard then a voice saying, Arise, ye dead, and come to judgment; and with that the rocks rent, the graves opened, and the dead that were therein came forth. Some of them were exceeding glad, and looked upward; and some sought to hide themselves under the mountains. Then I saw the man that sat upon the cloud open the book, and bid the world draw near. Yet there was, by reason of a fierce flame which issued out and came from before him, a convenient distance betwixt him and them, as betwixt the judge and the prisoners at the bar. I heard it also proclaimed to them that attended on the man that sat on the cloud, Gather together the tares, the chaff, and the stubble, and cast them into the burning lake. And with that, the bottomless pit opened, just whereabout I stood; out of the mouth of which there came, in an abundant manner, smoke and coals of fire, with hideous noises. It was also said to the same persons, Gather my wheat into the garner. And with that I saw many catched up and carried away into the clouds, but I was left behind. I also sought to hide myself, but I could not, for the man that sat upon the cloud still kept his eye upon me: my sins also came into my mind; and my conscience did accuse me on every side. Upon this I awaked from my sleep.

CHRISTIAN. But what was it that made you so afraid of this sight?

MAN. Why, I thought that the day of judgment was come, and that I was not ready for it: but this frighted me most, that the angels gathered up several, and left me behind; also the pit of hell opened her mouth just where I stood. My conscience too, afflicted me; and, as I thought, the Judge had always his eye upon me, showing indignation in his countenance.

Then said the Interpreter to Christian, Hast thou considered all these things?

CHRISTIAN. Yes, and they put me in hope and fear.

INTERPRETER. Well, keep all things so in thy mind that they may be as a goad in thy sides, to prick thee forward in the way thou must go. Then Christian began to gird up his loins, and to address himself to his journey. Then said the Interpreter, The Comforter be always with thee, good Christian, to guide thee in the way that leads to the City.

Now I saw in my dream, that the highway up which Christian was to go, was fenced on either side with a wall, and that wall was called Salvation. Up this way, therefore, did burdened Christian run, but not without great difficulty, because of the load on his back.

He ran thus till he came at a place somewhat ascending, and upon that place stood a cross, and a little below, in the bottom, a sepulchre. So I saw in my dream, that just as Christian came up with the cross, his burden loosed from off his shoulders, and fell from off his back, and began to tumble, and so continued to do, till it came to the mouth of the sepulchre, where it fell in, and I saw it no more.

Then was Christian glad and lightsome, and said, with a merry heart, He hath given me rest by his sorrow, and life by his death. Then he stood still awhile to look and wonder; for it was very surprising to him, that the sight of the cross should thus ease him of his burden. He looked, therefore, and looked again, even till the springs that were in his head sent the waters down his cheeks. Now, as he stood looking and weeping, behold three Shining Ones came to him and saluted him with Peace be to thee. So the first said to him, Thy sins be forgiven thee; the second stripped him of his rags and clothed him with change of raiment; the third also set a mark in his forehead, and gave him a roll with a seal upon it, which he bade him look on as he ran, and that he should give it in at the Celestial Gate. So they went their way.

I saw then in my dream, that he went on thus, even until he came at a bottom, where he saw, a little out of the way, three men fast asleep, with fetters upon their heels. The name of the one was Simple, another Sloth, and the third Presumption.

Christian then seeing them lie in this case, went to them, if peradventure he might awake them, and cried, You are like them that sleep on the top of a mast, for the Dead Sea is under you—a gulf that hath no bottom. Awake, therefore, and come away; be willing also, and I will help you off with your irons. He also told them, If he that goeth about like a roaring lion comes by, you will certainly become a prey to his teeth. With that they looked upon him, and began to reply in this sort: Simple said, I see no danger; Sloth said, Yet a little more sleep; and Presumption said, Every fat must stand upon its own bottom; what is the answer else that I should give thee? And so they lay down to sleep again, and Christian went on his way.

Yet was he troubled to think that men in that danger should so little esteem the kindness of him that so freely offered to help them, both by awakening of them, counselling of them, and proffering to help them off with their irons. And as he was troubled thereabout, he espied two men come tumbling over the wall, on the left hand of the narrow way; and they made up apace to him. The name of the one was Formalist, and the name of the other Hypocrisy. So, as I said, they drew up unto him, who thus entered with them into discourse.

CHRISTIAN. Gentlemen, whence came you, and whither go you?

FORMALIST and HYPROCRISY. We were born in the land of Vain-glory, and are going for praise to Mount Zion.

CHRISTIAN. Why came you not in at the gate, which standeth at the beginning of the way? Know you not that it is written, that he that cometh not in by the door, but climbeth up some other way, the same is a thief and a robber?

FORMALIST and HYPOCRISY. They said, That to go to the gate for entrance was, by all their countrymen, counted too far about; and that, therefore, their usual way was to make a short cut of it, and to climb over the wall, as they had done.

CHRISTIAN. But will it not be counted a trespass against the Lord of the city whither we are bound, thus to violate his revealed will?

FORMALIST and HYPOCRISY. They told him, that, as for that, he needed not to trouble his head thereabout; for what they did, they had custom for; and could produce, if need were, testimony that would witness it for more than a thousand years.

CHRISTIAN. But, said Christian, will your practice stand a trial at law?

FORMALIST and HYPOCRISY. They told him, That custom, it being of so long a standing as above a thousand years, would, doubtless, now be admitted as a thing legal by any impartial judge; and beside, said they, if we get into the way, what's matter which way we get in? if we are in, we are in; thou art but in the way, who, as we perceive, came in at the gate; and we are also in the way, that came tumbling over the wall; wherein, now is thy condition better than ours?

CHRISTIAN. I walk by the rule of my Master; you walk by the rude working of your fancies. You are counted thieves already, by the Lord of the way; therefore, I doubt you will not be found true men at the end of the way. You come in by yourselves, without his direction; and shall go out by yourselves, without his mercy.

To this they made him but little answer; only they bid him look to himself. Then I saw that they went on every man in his way, without much conference one with another; save that these two men told Christian, that as to laws and ordinances, they doubted not but they should as conscientiously do them as he; therefore, said they, we see not wherein thou differest from us, but by the coat that is on thy back, which was, as we trow, given thee by some of thy neighbours, to hide the shame of thy nakedness.

CHRISTIAN. By laws and ordinances you will not be saved, since you came not in by the door. And as for this coat that is on my back, it was given me by the Lord of the place whither I go; and that, as you say, to cover my nakedness with. And I take it as a token of his kindness to me; for I had nothing but rags before. And, besides, thus I comfort myself as I go: Surely, think I, when I come to the gate of the city, the Lord thereof will know me for good, since I have his coat on my back—a coat that he gave me freely in the day that he stripped me of my rags. I have, moreover, a mark in my forehead, of which, perhaps, you have taken no notice, which one of my Lord's most intimate associates fixed there in the day that my burden fell off my shoulders. I will tell you, moreover, that I had then given me a roll, sealed, to comfort me by reading, as I go on the way; I was also bid to give it in at the Celestial Gate, in token of my certain going in after it; all which things, I doubt, you want, and want them because you came not in at the gate.

To these things they gave him no answer; only they looked upon each

23

other, and laughed. Then I saw that they went on all, save that Christian kept before, who had no more talk but with himself, and that sometimes sighingly and sometimes comfortably; also he would be often reading in the roll that one of the Shining Ones gave him, by which he was refreshed.

I beheld, then, that they all went on till they came to the foot of the Hill Difficulty; at the bottom of which was a spring. There were also in the same place two other ways besides that which came straight from the gate; one turned to the left hand, and the other to the right, at the bottom of the hill; but the narrow way lay right up the hill, and the name of that going up the side of the hill is called Difficulty. Christian now went to the spring, and drank thereof, to refresh himself, and then began to go up the hill.

The other two also came to the foot of the hill; but when they saw that the hill was steep and high, and that there were two other ways to go; and supposing also, that these two ways might meet again, with that up which Christian went, on the other side of the hill; therefore they were resolved to go in those ways. Now the name of one of those ways was Danger, and the name of the other Destruction. So the one took the way which is called Danger, which led him into a great wood, and the other took directly up the way to Destruction, which led him into a wild field, full of dark mountains, where he stumbled and fell and rose no more.

I looked, then, after Christian, to see him go up the hill, where I perceived he fell from running to going, and from going to clambering upon his hands and his knees, because of the steepness of the place. Now, about the midway to the top of the hill was a pleasant arbour, made by the Lord of the hill for the refreshing of weary travellers; thither, therefore, Christian got, where also he sat down to rest him. Then he pulled his roll out of his bosom, and read therein to his comfort; he also now began afresh to take a review of the coat or garment that was given him as he stood by the cross. Thus pleasing himself awhile, he at last fell into a slumber, and thence into a fast sleep, which detained him in that place until it was almost night; and in his sleep his roll fell out of his hand. Now, as he was sleeping, there came one to him, and awaked him, saying, Go to the ant, thou sluggard; consider her ways, and be wise. And with that Christian suddenly started up, and sped him on his way, and went apace, till he came to the top of the hill.

Now, when he was got up to the top of the hill, there came two men running to meet him amain; the name of the one was Timorous, and of the other Mistrust; to whom Christian said, Sirs, what's the matter? You run the wrong way. Timorous answered, that they were going to the City of Zion, and had got up that difficult place; but, said he, the further we go, the more danger we meet with; wherefore we turned, and are going back again.

Yes, said Mistrust, for just before us lie a couple of lions in the way, whether sleeping or waking we know not, and we could not think, if we came within reach, but they would presently pull us in pieces.

CHRISTIAN. Then said Christian, You make me afraid, but whither shall I fly to be safe? If I go back to mine own country, *that* is prepared for fire and brimstone, and I shall certainly perish there. If I can get to the Celestial City, I am sure to be in safety there. I must venture. To go back is nothing but death; to go forward is fear of death, and life everlasting beyond it. I will yet go forward. So Mistrust and Timorous ran down the hill, and Christian went on his way. But, thinking again of what he heard from the men, he felt in his bosom for his roll, that he might read therein, and be comforted; but he felt, and found it not. Then was Christian in great distress, and knew not what to do; for he wanted that which used to relieve him, and that which should have been his pass into the Celestial City. Here, therefore, he began to be much perplexed, and knew not what to do. At last, he bethought himself, that he had slept in the arbour that is on the side of the hill; and, falling down upon his knees, he asked God forgiveness for that his foolish fact, and then went back to look for his roll. But all the way he went back, who can sufficiently set forth the sorrow of Christian's heart! Sometimes he sighed, sometimes he wept, and oftentimes he chid himself for being so foolish to fall asleep in that place, which was ejected only for a little refreshment for his weariness. Thus therefore he went back, carefully looking on this side, and on that, all the way as he went, if happily he might find his roll, that had been his comfort so many times in his journey. He went thus, till he came again within sight of the arbour where he sat and slept; but that sight renewed his sorrow the more, by bringing again, even afresh, his evil of sleeping into his mind. Thus, therefore, he now went on bewailing his sinful sleep, saying, O wretched man that I am! that I should sleep in the day-time! that I should sleep in the midst of difficulty! that I should so indulge the flesh, as to use that rest for ease to my flesh, which the Lord of the hill hath erected only for the relief of the spirits of pilgrims!

How many steps have I took in vain! Thus it happened to Israel, for their sin; they were sent back again by the way of the Red Sea; and I am made to tread those steps with sorrow, which I might have trod with delight, had it not been for this sinful sleep. How far might I have been on my way by this time! I am made to read those steps thrice over, which I needed not to have trod but once; yea, now also I am like to be benighted, for the day is almost spent. O that I had not slept!

Now by this time he was come to the arbour again, where for a while he sat down and wept; but at last, as Christian would have it, looking sorrowfully down under the settle, there he espied his roll; the which he, with trembling and haste, catched up, and put it into his bosom. But who can tell how joyful this man was when he had gotten his roll again! for this roll was the assurance of his life and acceptance at the desired haven. Therefore he laid it up in his bosom, gave thanks to God for directing his eye to the place where it lay, and with joy and tears betook himself again to his journey. But O, how nimbly now did he go up the rest of the hill! Yet, before he got up, the sun went down upon Christian; and this made

25

him again recall the vanity of his sleeping to his remembrance; and thus he again began to condole with himself. O thou sinful sleep! how, for thy sake am I like to be benighted in my journey! I must walk without the sun; darkness must cover the path of my feet; and I must hear the noise of the doleful creatures, because of my sinful sleep. Now also he remembered the story that Mistrust and Timorous told him of, how they were frighted with the sight of the lions. Then said Christian to himself again, These beasts range in the night for their prey; and if they should meet with me in the dark, how should I shift them? How should I escape being by them torn in pieces? Thus he went on his way. But while he was thus bewailing his unhappy miscarriage, he lift up his eyes, and behold there was a very stately palace before him, the name of which was Beautiful; and it stood just by the highway side.

So I saw in my dream, that he made haste and went forward, that if possible he might get lodging there. Now before he had gone far, he entered into a very narrow passage, which was about a furlong off the porter's lodge; and looking very narrowly before him as he went, he espied two lions in the way. Now, thought he, I see the dangers that Mistrust and Timorous were driven back by. (The lions were chained, but he saw not the chains.) Then he was afraid, and thought also himself to go back after them, for he thought nothing but death was before him. But the porter at at the lodge, whose name is Watchful, perceiving that Christian made a halt as if he would go back, cried unto him, saying, Is thy strength so small? Fear not the lions, for they are chained, and are placed there for trial of faith where it is, and for discovery of those that have none. Keep in the midst of the path, and no hurt shall come unto thee.

Then I saw that he went on, trembling for fear of the lions, but taking good heed to the directions of the porter; he heard them roar, but they did him no harm. Then he clapped his hands, and went on till he came and stood before the gate, where the porter was. Then said Christian to the porter, Sir, what house is this? and may I lodge here tonight? The porter answered, This house was built by the Lord of the hill, and he built it for the relief and security of pilgrims. The porter also asked whence he was, and whither he was going.

CHRISTIAN. I am come from the City of Destruction, and am going to Mount Zion; but because the sun is now set, I desire, if I may, to lodge here tonight.

PORTER. What is your name?

CHRISTIAN. My name is now Christian, but my name at the first was Graceless; I came of the race of Japheth, whom God will persuade to dwell in the tents of Shem.

PORTER. But how doth it happen that you come so late? The sun is set.

CHRISTIAN. I had been here sooner, but that, wretched man that I am! I slept in the arbour that stands on the hill-side; nay, I had, notwithstanding that, been here much sooner, but that, in my sleep, I lost my evidence, and came without it to the brow of the hill; and then feeling for it, and finding it not, I was forced, with sorrow of heart, to go back to the place where I slept my sleep, where I found it, and now I am come.

PORTER. Well, I will call out one of the virgins of this place, who will, if she likes your talk, bring you into the rest of the family, according to the rules of the house. So Watchful, the porter, rang a bell, at the sound of which came out at the door of the house, a grave and beautiful damsel, named Discretion, and asked why she was called.

The porter answered, This man is in a journey from the City of Destruction to Mount Zion, but being weary and benighted, he asked me if he might lodge here tonight; so I told him I would call for thee, who, after discourse had with him, mayest do as seemeth thee good, even according to the law of the house.

Then she asked him whence he was, and whither he was going; and he told her. She asked him also how he got into the way; and he told her. Then she asked him what he had seen and met with in the way; and he told her. And last she asked his name; so he said, It is Christian, and I have so much the more a desire to lodge here tonight, because, by what I perceive, this place was built by the Lord of the hill, for the relief and security of pilgrims. So she smiled, but the water stood in her eyes; and after a little pause, she said, I will call forth two or three more of the family. So she ran to the door, and called out Prudence, Piety, and Charity, who, after a little more discourse with him, had him into the family; and many of them meeting him at the threshold of the house, said, Come in, thou blessed of the Lord; this house was built by the Lord of the hill, on purpose to entertain such pilgrims in. Then he bowed his head, and followed them into the house. So when he was come in and sat down, they gave him something to drink, and consented together, that until supper was ready, some of them should have some particular discourse with Christian, for the best improvement of time; and they appointed Piety, and Prudence, and Charity to discourse with him; and thus they began:

PIETY. Come, good Christian, since we have been so loving to you, to receive you into our house this night, let us, if perhaps we may better ourselves thereby, talk with you of all things that have happened to you in your pilgrimage.

CHRISTIAN. With a very good will, and I am glad that you are so well disposed.

PIETY. What moved you at first to betake yourself to a pilgrim's life?

CHRISTIAN. I was driven out of my native country, by a dreadful sound that was in mine ears; to wit, that unavoidable destruction did attend me, if I abode in that place where I was.

PIETY. But how did it happen that you came out of your country this way?

CHRISTIAN. It was as God would have it; for when I was under the fears of destruction, I did not know whither to go; but by chance there came a man, even to me, as I was trembling and weeping, whose name is Evangelist, and he directed me to the wicket-gate, which else I should never have found, and so set me into the way that hath led me directly to this house.

PIETY. But did you not come by the house of the Interpreter?

CHRISTIAN. Yes, and did see such things there, the remembrance of which will stick by me as long as I live; especially three things, to wit, how Christ, in despite of Satan, maintains his work of grace in the heart; how the man had sinned himself quite out of hopes of God's mercy; and also the dream of him that thought in his sleep the day of judgment was come.

PIETY. Why, did you hear him tell his dream?

CHRISTIAN. Yes, and a dreadful one it was. I thought it made my heart ache as he was telling of it; but yet I am glad I heard it.

PIETY. Was that all that you saw at the house of the Interpreter?

CHRISTIAN. No; he took me and had me where he showed me a stately palace, and how the people were clad in gold that were in it; and how there came a venturous man and cut his way through the armed men that stood in the door to keep him out; and how he was bid to come in, and win eternal glory. Methought those things did ravish my heart! I would have staid at that good man's house a twelvemonth, but that I knew I had further to go.

PIETY. And what saw you else in the way?

CHRISTIAN. Saw! why, I went but a little further, and I saw one, as I thought in my mind, hang bleeding upon the tree; and the very sight of him made my burden fall off my back (for I groaned under a very heavy burden), but then it fell down from off me. It was a strange thing to me, for I never saw such a thing before; yea, and while I stood looking up, for then I could not forbear looking, three Shining Ones came to me. One of them testified that my sins were forgiven me; another stripped me of my rags, and gave me this broidered coat which you see; and the third set the mark which you see in my forehead, and gave me this sealed roll. (And with that he plucked it out of his bosom.)

PIETY. But you saw more than this, did you not?

CHRISTIAN. The things that I have told you were the best, yet some other matters I saw, as, namely, I saw three men, Simple, Sloth, and Presumption, lie asleep a little out of the way, as I came, with irons upon their heels; but do you think I could awake them? I also saw Formality and Hypocrisy come tumbling over the wall, to go, as they pretended, to Zion, but they were quickly lost, even as I myself did tell them; but they would not believe. But above all, I found it hard work to get up this hill, and as hard to come by the lions' mouths; and truly if it had not been for the good man, the porter that stands at the gate, I do not know but that after all I might have gone back again; but now, I thank God I am here, and I thank you for receiving of me.

Then Prudence thought good to ask him a few questions, and desired his answer to them.

PRUDENCE. Do you not think sometimes of the country from whence you came?

CHRISTIAN. Yes, but with much shame and detestation: truly if I had been mindful of that country from whence I came out, I might have had opportunity to have returned; but now I desire a better country, that is, an heavenly.

PRUDENCE. Do you not yet bear away with you some of the things that then you were conversant withal?

CHRISTIAN. Yes, but greatly against my will; especially my inward and carnal cogitations, with which all my countrymen, as well as myself, were delighted; but now all those things are my grief; and might I but choose mine own things, I would choose never to think of those things more; but when I would be doing of that which is best, that which is worst is with me.

PRUDENCE. Do you not find sometimes, as if those things were vanquished, which at other times are your perplexity?

CHRISTIAN. Yes, but that is but seldom; but they are to me golden hours, in which such things happen to me.

PRUDENCE. Can you remember by what means you find your annoyances, at times, as if they were vanquished?

CHRISTIAN. Yes; when I think what I saw at the cross, that will do it; and when I look upon my broidered coat, that will do it; also when I look into the roll that I carry in my bosom, that will do it; and when my thoughts wax warm about whither I am going, that will do it.

PRUDENCE. And what is it that makes you so desirous to go to Mount Zion?

CHRISTIAN. Why, there I hope to see him alive that did hang dead on the cross; and there I hope to be rid of all those things that to this day are in me an annoyance to me; there, they say, there is no death; and there I shall dwell with such company as I like best. For, to tell you truth, I love him, because I was by him eased of my burden; and I am weary of my inward sickness. I would fain be where I shall die no more, and with the company that shall continually cry, Holy, holy, holy.

Then said Charity to Christian, Have you a family? Are you a married man?

CHRISTIAN. I have a wife and four small children.

CHARITY. And why did you not bring them along with you?

CHRISTIAN. Then Christian wept, and said, O how willingly would I have done it! but they were all of them utterly averse to my going on pilgrimage.

CHARITY. But you should have talked to them, and have endeavoured to have shown them the danger of being behind.

CHRISTIAN. So I did; and told them also what God had shown to me of the destruction of our city; but I seemed to them as one mocked, and they believed me not.

CHARITY. And did you pray to God that he would bless your counsel to them?

CHRISTIAN. Yes, and that with much affection; for you must think that my wife and poor children were very dear unto me.

29

CHARITY. But did you tell them of your own sorrow, and fear of destruction? for I suppose that destruction was visible enough to you.

CHRISTIAN. Yes, over, and over, and over. They might also see my fears in my countenance, in my tears, and also in my trembling under the apprehension of the judgment that did hang over our heads; but all was not sufficient to prevail with them to come with me.

CHARITY. But what could they say for themselves, why they came not?

CHRISTIAN. Why, my wife was afraid of losing this world, and my children were given to the foolish delights of youth; so what by one thing, and what by another, they left me to wander in this manner alone.

CHARITY. But did you not, with your vain life, damp all that you by words used by way of persuasion to bring them away with you?

CHRISTIAN. Indeed, I cannot commend my life; for I am conscious to myself of many failings therein; I know also, that a man by his conversation may soon overthrow, what by argument or persuasion he doth labour to fasten upon others for their good. Yet this I can say, I was very wary of giving them occasion, by any unseemly action, to make them averse to going on pilgrimage. Yea, for this very thing, they would tell me I was too precise, and that I denied myself of things, for their sakes, in which they saw no evil. Nay, I think I may say, that if what they saw in me did hinder them, it was my great tenderness in sinning against God, or of doing any wrong to my neighbour.

CHARITY. Indeed Cain hated his brother, because his own works were evil, and his brother's righteous; and if thy wife and children have been offended with thee for this, they thereby show themselves to be implacable to good, and thou hast delivered thy soul from their blood.

Now I saw in my dream, that thus they sat talking together until supper was ready. So when they had made ready, they sat down to meat. Now the table was furnished with fat things, and with wine that was well refined: and all their talk at the table was about the Lord of the hill; as, namely, about what he had done, and wherefore he did what he did, and why he had builded that house. And by what they said, I perceived that he had been a great warrior, and had fought with and slain him that had the power of death, but not without great danger to himself, which made me love him the more.

For, as they said, and as I believe (said Christian), he did it with the loss of much blood; but that which put glory of grace into all he did, was, that he did it out of pure love to his country. And besides, there were some of them of the household that said they had seen and spoke with him since he did die on the cross; and they have attested that they had it from his own lips, that he is such a lover of poor pilgrims, that the like is not to be found from the east to the west.

They, moreover, gave an instance of what they affirmed, and that was, he had stripped himself of his glory, that he might do this for the poor; and that they heard him say and affirm, that he would not dwell in the mountain of Zion alone. They said, moreover, that he had made many pilgrims

30

princes, though by nature they were beggars born, and their original had been the dunghill.

Thus they discoursed together till late at night; and after they had committed themselves to their Lord for protection, they betook themselves to rest: the Pilgrim they laid in a large upper chamber, whose window opened toward the sunrising; the name of the chamber was Peace; where he slept till break of day, and then he awoke and sang:

> Where am I now? Is this the love and care
> Of Jesus for the men that pilgrims are?
> Thus to provide! that I should be forgiven!
> And dwell already the next door to heaven!

So, in the morning, they all got up; and after some more discourse, they told him that he should not depart till they had shown him the rarities of that place. And first, they had him into the study, where they showed him records of the greatest antiquity; in which, as I remember my dream, they showed him first the pedigree of the Lord of the hill, that he was the son of the Ancient of Days, and came by that eternal generation. Here also was more fully recorded the acts that he had done, and the names of many hundreds that he had taken into his service; and how he had placed them in such habitations, that could neither by length of days, nor decays of nature, be dissolved.

Then they read to him some of the worthy acts that some of his servants had done: as, how they had subdued kingdoms, wrought righteousness, obtained promises, stopped the mouths of lions, quenched the violence of fire, escaped the edge of the sword, out of weakness were made strong, waxed valiant in fight, and turned to flight the armies of the aliens.

They then read again in another part of the records of the house, where it was showed how willing their Lord was to receive into his favour any, even any, though they in time had offered great affronts to his person and proceedings. Here also were several other histories of many other famous things, of all which Christian had a view; as of things both ancient and modern; together with prophecies and predictions of things that have their certain accomplishment, both to the dread and amazement of enemies, and the comfort and solace of pilgrims.

The next day they took him and had him into the armoury, where they showed him all manner of furniture, which their Lord had provided for pilgrims, as sword, shield, helmet, breastplate, all-prayer, and shoes that would not wear out. And there was here enough of this to harness out as many men, for the services of their Lord, as there be stars in the heaven for multitude.

They also showed him some of the engines with which some of his servants had done wonderful things. They showed him Moses' rod; the hammer and nail with which Jael slew Sisera; the pitchers, trumpets, and lamps too, with which Gideon put to flight the armies of Midian. Then they showed him the ox's goad wherewith Shamgar slew six hundred men. They showed him, also, the jawbone with which Samson did such mighty feats. They showed him, moreover, the sling and stone with which David slew Goliath of Gath; and the sword, also, with which their Lord will kill the Man of Sin, in the day that he shall rise up to the prey. They showed him, besides, many excellent things, with which Christian was much delighted. This done, they went to their rest again.

Then I saw in my dream, that, on the morrow, he got up to go forward; but they desired him to stay till the next day also; and then, said they, we will, if the day be clear, show you the Delectable Mountains, which, they said, would yet further add to his comfort, because they were nearer the desired haven than the place where at present he was; so he consented and staid. When the morning was up, they had him to the top of the house, and bid him look south; so he did; and, behold, at a great distance, he saw a most pleasant mountainous country, beautified with woods, vineyards, fruits of all sorts, flowers also, with springs ..ʳ ...ntains, very delectable to behold. Then he asked the name of the country. They said it was Immanuel's Land; and it is as common, said they, as this hill is, to and for all the pilgrims. And when thou comest there, from thence, said they, thou mayest see to the gate of the Celestial City, as the shepherds that live there will make appear.

Now, he bethought himself of setting forward, and they were willing he should. But first, said they, let us go again into the armoury. So they did; and when they came there, they harnessed him from head to foot with what was of proof, lest, perhaps, he should meet with assaults in the way. He being, therefore, thus accoutred, walketh out with his friends to the gate, and there he asked the porter if he saw any pilgrims pass by. Then the porter answered, Yes.

CHRISTIAN. Pray, did you know him? said he.

PORTER. I asked his name, and he told me it was Faithful.

CHRISTIAN. O, said Christian, I know him; he is my townsman, my near neighbour; he comes from the place where I was born. How far do you think he may be before?

PORTER. He is got by this time below the hill.

CHRISTIAN. Well, said Christian, good Porter, the Lord be with thee, and add to all thy blessings much increase, for the kindness that thou hast showed to me.

Then he began to go forward; but Discretion, Piety, Charity, and Prudence, would accompany him down to the foot of the hill. So they went on together, reiterating their former discourses, till they came to go down the hill. Then, said Christian, as it was difficult coming up, so, so far as I can see, it is dangerous going down. Yes, said Prudence, so it is, for it is a hard matter for a man to go down into the Valley of Humiliation, as thou art now, and to catch no slip by the way; therefore, said they, are we come out to accompany thee down the hill. So he began to go down, but very warily; yet he caught a slip or two.

32

Then I saw in my dream that these good companions, when Christian was gone to the bottom of the hill, gave him a loaf of bread, a bottle of wine, and a cluster of raisins; and then he went on his way.

But now, in this Valley of Humiliation, poor Christian was hard put to it; for he had gone but a little way, before he espied a foul fiend coming over the field to meet him; his name is Apollyon. Then did Christian begin to be afraid, and to cast in his mind whether to go back or to stand his ground. But he considered again that he had no armour for his back; and, therefore, thought that to turn the back to him might give him the greater advantage, with ease to pierce him with his darts. Therefore he resolved to venture and stand his ground; for, thought he, had I no more in mine eye than the saving of my life, it would be the best way to stand.

So he went on, and Apollyon met him. Now the monster was hideous to behold; he was cloathed with scales, like a fish (and they are his pride), he had wings like a dragon, feet like a bear, and out of his belly came fire and smoke, and his mouth was as the mouth of a lion. When he was come up to Christian, he beheld him with a disdainful countenance, and thus began to question with him.

APPOLLYON. Whence come you? and whither are you bound?

CHRISTIAN. I am come from the City of Destruction, which is the place of all evil, and am going to the City of Zion.

APOLLYON. By this I perceive thou art one of my subjects, for all that country is mine, and I am the prince and god of it. How is it, then, that thou hast run away from thy king? Were it not that I hope thou mayest do me more service, I would strike thee now, at one blow, to the ground.

CHRISTIAN. I was born, indeed, in your dominions, but your service was hard, and your wages such as a man could not live on, for the wages of sin is death; therefore, when I was come to years, I did as other considerate persons do, look out, if, perhaps, I might mend myself.

APOLLYON. There is no prince that will thus lightly lose his subjects, neither will I as yet lose thee; but since thou complainest of thy service and wages, be content to go back; what our country will afford, I do here promise to give thee.

CHRISTIAN. But I have let myself to another, even to the King of princes; and how can I, with fairness, go back with thee?

APOLLYON. Thou hast done in this according to the proverb, changed a bad for a worse; but it is ordinary for those that have professed themselves his servants, after a while to give him the slip, and return again to me. Do thou so too, and all shall be well.

CHRISTIAN. I have given him my faith, and sworn my allegiance to him; how, then, can I go back from this, and not be hanged as a traitor?

APOLLYON. Thou didst the same to me, and yet I am willing to pass by all, if now thou wilt yet turn again and go back.

CHRISTIAN. What I promised thee was in my nonage; and, besides, I count the Prince under whose banner now I stand is able to absolve me;

yea, and to pardon also what I did as to my compliance with thee; and besides, O thou destroying Apollyon! to speak truth, I like his service, his wages, his servants, his government, his company, and country, better than thine; and, therefore, leave off to persuade me further; I am his servant, and I will follow him.

APOLLYON. Consider again, when thou art in cool blood, what thou art like to meet with in the way that thou goest. Thou knowest that, for the most part, his servants come to an ill end, because they are transgressors against me and my ways. How many of them have been put to shameful deaths! and, besides, thou countest his service better than mine, whereas he never came yet from the place where he is to deliver any that served him out of their hands; but as for me, how many times, as all the world very well knows, have I delivered, either by power or fraud, those that have faithfully served me, from him and his, though taken by them; and so I will deliver thee.

CHRISTIAN. His forbearing at present to deliver them is on purpose to try their love, whether they will cleave to him to the end; and as for the ill end thou sayest they come to, that is most glorious in their account; for, for present deliverance, they do not much expect it, for they stay for their glory, and then they shall have it, when their Prince comes in his and the glory of the angels.

APOLLYON. Thou hast already been unfaithful in thy service to him; and how dost thou think to receive wages of him?

CHRISTIAN. Wherein, O Apollyon! have I been unfaithful to him?

APOLLYON. Thou didst faint at first setting out, when thou wast almost choked in the Gulf of Dispond; thou didst attempt wrong ways to be rid of thy burden, whereas thou shouldest have stayed till thy Prince had taken it off; thou didst sinfully sleep, and lose thy choice thing; thou wast, also, almost persuaded to go back, at the sight of the lions; and when thou talkest of thy journey, and of what thou hast heard and seen, thou art inwardly desirous of vain-glory in all that thou sayest or doest.

CHRISTIAN. All this is true, and much more which thou hast left out; but the Prince, whom I serve and honour, is merciful, and ready to forgive; but, besides, these infirmities possessed me in thy country, for there I sucked them in; and I have groaned under them, been sorry for them, and have obtained pardon of my Prince.

APOLLYON. Then Apollyon broke out into a grievous rage, saying, I am an enemy to this Prince; I hate his person, his laws, and people; I am come out on purpose to withstand thee.

CHRISTIAN. Apollyon, beware what you do; for I am in the king's highway, the way of holiness; therefore take heed to yourself.

APOLLYON. Then Apollyon straddled quite over the whole breadth of the way, and said, I am void of fear in this matter: prepare thyself to die; for I swear by my infernal den, that thou shalt go no farther; here will I spill thy soul.

And with that he threw a flaming dart at his breast; but Christian had a

34

shield in his hand, with which he caught it, and so prevented the danger of that.

Then did Christian draw; for he saw it was time to bestir him: and Apollyon as fast made at him, throwing darts as thick as hail; by the which, notwithstanding all that Christian could do to avoid it, Apollyon wounded him in his head, his hand, and foot. This made Christian give a little back; Apollyon, therefore, followed his work amain, and Christian again took courage, and resisted as manfully as he could. This sore combat lasted for above half a day, even till Christian was almost quite spent; for you must know, that Christian, by reason of his wounds, must needs grow weaker and weaker.

Then Apollyon, espying his opportunity, began to gather up close to Christian, and wrestling with him, gave him a dreadful fall; and with that, Christian's sword flew out of his hand. Then said Apollyon, I am sure of thee now. And with that he had almost pressed him to death; so that Christian began to despair of life: but as God would have it, while Apollyon was fetching of his last blow, thereby to make a full end of this good man, Christian nimbly stretched out his hand for his sword, and caught it, saying, Rejoice not against me, O mine enemy: when I fall, I shall rise; and with that gave him a deadly thrust, which made him give back, as one that had received his mortal wound. Christian perceiving that, made at him again, saying, Nay, in all these things we are more than conquerors, through him that loved us. And with that Apollyon spread forth his dragon's wings, and sped him away, that Christian for a season saw him no more.

Now, at the end of this valley, was another, called the Valley of the Shadow of Death, and Christian must needs go through it, because the way to the Celestial City lay through the midst of it. Now this valley is a very solitary place. The prophet Jeremiah thus describes it: A wilderness, a land of deserts, and of pits, a land of drought, and of the shadow of death, a land that no man (but a Christian) passed through, and where no man dwelt.

Now here Christian was worse put to it than in his fight with Apollyon; as by the sequel you shall see.

I saw then in my dream, that when Christian was got to the borders of the Shadow of Death, there met him two men, children of them that brought up an evil report of the good land, making haste to go back; to whom Christian spake as follows:

CHRISTIAN. Whither are you going?

MEN. They said, Back! back! and we would have you to do so too, if either life or peace is prized by you.

CHRISTIAN. Why? what's the matter? said Christian.

MEN. Matter! said they; we were going that way as you are going, and went as far as we durst; and indeed we were almost past coming back; for had we gone a little further we had not been here to bring the news to thee.

CHRISTIAN. But what have you met with? said Christian.

MEN. Why, we were almost in the Valley of the Shadow of Death; but that, by good hap, we looked before us, and saw the danger before we came to it.

CHRISTIAN. But what have you seen? said Christian.

MEN. Seen! Why, the valley itself, which is as dark as pitch; we also saw there the hobgoblins, satyrs, and dragons of the pit; we heard also in that valley a continual howling and yelling as of a people under unutterable misery, who there sat bound in affliction and irons; and over that valley hang the discouraging clouds of confusion. Death also doth always spread his wings over it. In a word, it is every whit dreadful, being utterly without order.

CHRISTIAN. Then said Christian, I perceive not yet, by what you have said, but that this is my way to the desired haven.

MEN. Be it thy way; we will not choose it for ours. So they parted, and Christian went on his way, but still with his sword drawn in his hand; for fear lest he should be assaulted.

I saw then in my dream so far as this valley reached, there was on the right hand a very deep ditch: that ditch is it into which the blind have led the blind in all ages, and have both miserably perished. Again, behold, on the left hand, there was a very dangerous quag, into which, if even a good man falls, he can find not bottom for his foot to stand on. Into that quag king David once did fall, and had no doubt therein been smothered, had not He that is able pluckt him out.

The pathway was here also exceedingly narrow, and therefore good Christian was the more put to it; for when he sought, in the dark, to shun the ditch on the one hand, he was ready to tip over into the mire on the other; also when he sought to escape the mire, without great carefulness he would be ready to fall into the ditch. Thus he went on, and I heard him here sigh bitterly; for besides the dangers mentioned above, the pathway was here so dark, that oft-times, when he lift up his foot to set forward, he knew not where, or upon what he should set it next.

About the midst of this valley, I perceived the mouth of hell to be, and it stood also hard by the way-side. Now, thought Christian, what shall I do? And ever and anon the flame and smoke would come out in such abundance, with sparks and hideous noises (things that cared not for Christian's sword, as did Apollyon before), that he was forced to put up his sword, and betake himself to another weapon, called All-prayer. So he cried in my hearing, O Lord, I beseech thee, deliver my soul! Thus he went on a great while, yet still the flames would be reaching towards him. Also he heard doleful voices, and rushings to and fro, so that sometimes he thought he should be torn in pieces, or trodden down like mire in the streets. This frightful sight was seen, and these dreadful noises were heard by him for several miles together. And, coming to a place, where he thought he heard a company of fiends coming forward to meet him, he stopped and began to muse what he had best to do. Sometimes he had half a thought to go back; then again he thought he might be half way through the valley;

he remembered also how he had already vanquished many a danger, and that the danger of going back might be much more than for to go forward; so he resolved to go on. Yet the fiends seemed to come nearer and nearer; but when they were come even almost at him, he cried out with a most vehement voice, I will walk in the strength of the Lord God; so they gave back, and came no farther.

One thing I would not let slip; I took notice that now poor Christian was so confounded, that he did not know his own voice; and thus I perceived it. Just when he was come over against the mouth of the burning pit, one of the wicked ones got behind him, and stept up softly to him, and, whisperingly, suggested many grievous blasphemies to him, which he verily thought had proceeded from his own mind. This put Christian more to it than anything that he met with before; even to think that he should now blaspheme him that he loved so much before; yet, if he could have helped it, he would not have done it; but he had not the discretion either to stop his ears, or to know from whence these blasphemies came.

When Christian had travelled in this disconsolate condition some considerable time, he thought he heard the voice of a man, as going before him, saying, Though I walk through the valley of the shadow of death, I will fear no evil; for thou art with me.

Then he was glad, and that for these reasons:

First, Because he gathered from thence, that some who feared God, were in this valley as well as himself.

Secondly, For that he perceived God was with them, though in that dark and dismal state; and why not, thought he, with me? though, by reason of the impediment that attends this place, I cannot perceive it.

Thirdly, For that he hoped, could he overtake them, to have company by and by. So he went on, and called to him that was before; but he knew not what to answer; for that he also thought himself to be alone. And by and by the day broke; then said Christian, He hath turned the shadow of death into the morning.

Now morning being come, he looked back, not out of desire to return, but to see, by the light of the day, what hazards he had gone through in the dark. So he saw more perfectly the ditch that was on the one hand, and the quag that was on the other; also how narrow the way was which led betwixt them both; also now he saw the hobgoblins, and satyrs, and dragons of the pit, but all afar off (for after break of day, they came not nigh); yet they were discovered to him, according to that which is written, He discovereth deep things out of darkness, and bringeth out to light the shadow of death.

Now was Christian much affected with his deliverance from all the dangers of his solitary way; which dangers, though he feared them more before, yet he saw them more clearly now, because the light of the day made them conspicuous to him. And about this time the sun was rising, and this was another mercy to Christian; for you must note, that though the first part of the Valley of the Shadow of Death was dangerous, yet this second part which he was yet to go, was, if possible far more dangerous: for from the place where he now stood, even to the end of the valley, the way was all along set so full of snares, traps, gins, and nets here, and so full of pits, pitfalls, deep holes, and shelvings down there, that had it now been dark, as it was when he came the first part of the way, had he had a thousand souls, they had in reason been cast away; but, as I said, just now the sun was rising. Then said he, His candle shineth upon my head, and by his light I walk through darkness.

In this light, therefore, he came to the end of the valley. Now I saw in my dream, that at the end of this valley lay blood, bones, ashes, and mangled bodies of men, even of pilgrims that had gone this way formerly; and while I was musing what should be the reason, I espied a little before me a cave, where two giants, Pope and Pagan, dwelt in old time; by whose power and tyranny the men whose bones, blood, ashes, etc., lay there, were cruelly put to death. But by this place Christian went without much danger, whereat I somewhat wondered; but I have learnt since, that Pagan has been dead many a day; and as for the other, though he be yet alive, he is, by reason of age, and also of the many shrewd brushes that he met with in his younger days, grown so crazy and stiff in his joints, that he can now do little more than sit in his cave's mouth, grinning at pilgrims as they go by, and biting his nails because he cannot come at them.

So I saw that Christian went on his way; yet, at the sight of the Old Man that sat in the mouth of the cave, he could not tell what to think, especially because he spake to him, though he could not go after him; saying, You will never mend, till more of you be burned. But he held his peace, and set a good face on it, and so went by and catched no hurt.

Now, as Christian went on his way, he came to a little ascent, which was cast up on purpose, that pilgrims might see before them. Up there, therefore, Christian went; and looking forward, he saw Faithful before him, upon his journey. Then said Christian aloud, Ho! ho! Soho! stay, and I will be your companion. At that, Faithful looked behind him; to whom Christian cried again, Stay, stay, till I come up to you. But Faithful answered. No, I am upon my life, and the Avenger of Blood is behind me.

At this, Christian was somewhat moved, and putting to all his strength, he quickly got up with Faithful, and did also overrun him; so the last was first. Then did Christian vaingloriously smile, because he had gotten the start of his brother; but not taking good heed to his feet, he suddenly stumbled and fell, and could not rise again, until Faithful came up to help him.

Then I saw in my dream, they went very lovingly on together, and had sweet discourse of all things that had happened to them in their pilgrimage; and thus Christian began.

CHRISTIAN. My honoured and well-beloved brother, Faithful, I am glad that I have overtaken you; and that God has so tempered our spirits, that we can walk as companions in this so pleasant a path.

FAITHFUL. I had thought, dear friend, to have had your company quite from our town; but you did get the start of me, wherefore I was forced to come thus much of the way alone.

CHRISTIAN. How long did you stay in the City of Destruction, before you set out after me on your pilgrimage?

FAITHFUL. Till I could stay no longer; for there was great talk presently after you were gone out, that our city would, in short time, with fire from heaven, be burned down to the ground.

CHRISTIAN. What! did your neighbours talk so?

FAITHFUL. Yes, it was for a while in everybody's mouth.

CHRISTIAN. What! and did no more of them but you come out to escape the danger?

FAITHFUL. Though there was, as I said, a great talk thereabout, yet I do not think they did firmly believe it. For in the heat of the discourse, I heard some of them deridingly speak of you, and of your desperate journey (for so they called this your pilgrimage), but I did believe, and do still, that the end of our city will be with fire and brimstone from above; and therefore I have made my escape.

CHRISTIAN. Did you hear no talk of neighbour Pliable?

FAITHFUL. Yes, Christian, I heard that he followed you till he came at the Slough of Dispond, where, as some said, he fell in; but he would not be known to have so done; but I am sure he was soundly bedabbled with that kind of dirt.

CHRISTIAN. And what said the neighbours to him?

FAITHFUL. He hath, since his going back, been greatly in derision, and that among all sorts of people; some do mock and despise him; and scarce will any set him on work. He is now seven times worse than if he had never gone out of the city.

CHRISTIAN. But why should they be so set against him, since they also despise the way that he forsook?

FAITHFUL. O! they say, Hang him, he is a turn-coat; he was not true to his profession. I think God has stirred up even his enemies to hiss at him, and make him a proverb, because he hath forsaken the way.

CHRISTIAN. Had you no talk with him before you came out?

FAITHFUL. I met him once in the streets, but he leered away on the other side, as one ashamed of what he had done; so I spake not to him.

CHRISTIAN. Well, at my first-setting out, I had hopes of that man; but now I fear he will perish in the overthrow of the city; for it is happened to him according to the true proverb, The dog is turned to his own vomit again; and the sow that was washed, to her wallowing in the mire.

FAITHFUL. These are my fears of him too; but who can hinder that which will be?

CHRISTIAN. Well, neighbour Faithful, said Christian, let us leave him, and talk of things that more immediately concern ourselves. Tell me now, what you have met with in the way as you came; for I know you have met with some things, or else it may be writ for a wonder.

FAITHFUL. I escaped the Slough that I perceived you fell into, and got up to the gate without that danger.

CHRISTIAN. Did you meet with no assault as you came?

FAITHFUL When I came to the foot of the hill called Difficulty, I met with a very aged man, who asked me what I was, and whither bound. I told him that I am a pilgrim, going to the Celestial City. Then said the old man, Thou lookest like an honest fellow; wilt thou be content to dwell with me for the wages that I shall give thee? Then I asked him his name, and where he dwelt. He said his name was Adam the First, and that he dwelt in the town of Deceit. I asked him then, what was his work, and what the wages that he would give. He told me, that his work was many delights; and his wages, that I should be his heir at last. I further asked him what house he kept, and what other servants he had. So he told me, that his house was maintained with all the dainties in the world; and that his servants were those of his own begetting. Then I asked how many children he had. He said that he had but three daughters; the Lust of the Flesh, the Lust of the Eyes, and the Pride of Life, and that I should marry them all if I would. Then I asked how long time he would have me live with him? And he told me, As long as he lived himself.

CHRISTIAN. Well, and what conclusion came the old man and you to, at last?

FAITHFUL. Why, at first, I found myself somewhat inclinable to go with the man, for I thought he spake very fair; but looking in his forehead, as I talked with him, I saw there written, Put off the old man with his deeds.

CHRISTIAN And how then?

FAITHFUL. Then it came burning hot into my mind, whatever he said, and however he flattered, when he got me home to his house, he would sell me for a slave. So I bid him forbear to talk, for I would not come near the door of his house. Then he reviled me, and told me, that he would send such a one after me, that should make my way bitter to my soul. So I turned to go away from him; but just as I turned myself to go thence, I felt him take hold of my flesh, and give me such a deadly twitch back, that I thought he had pulled part of me after himself. This made me cry, O wretched man! So I went on my way up the hill.

Now when I had got about half way up, I looked behind, and saw one coming after me, swift as the wind; so he overtook me just about the place where the settle stands.

CHRISTIAN. Just there, said Christian, did I sit down to rest me; but being overcome with sleep, I there lost this roll out of my bosom.

FAITHFUL. But, good brother, hear me out. So soon as the man overtook me, he was but a word and a blow, for down he knocked me, and laid me for dead. But when I was a little come to myself again, I asked him wherefore he served me so. He said, because of my secret inclining to Adam the First: and with that he struck me another deadly blow on the breast, and beat me down backward; so I lay at his foot as dead as before. So, when I came to myself again, I cried him mercy; but he said, I know not how to show mercy; and with that knocked me down again. He had doubtless made an end of me, but that one came by, and bid him forbear.

CHRISTIAN. Who was that that bid him forbear?

FAITHFUL. I did not know him at first, but as he went by, I perceived the holes in his hands, and in his side; then I concluded that he was our Lord. So I went up the hill.

CHRISTIAN. That man that overtook you was Moses. He spareth none, neither knoweth he how to show mercy to those that transgress his law.

FAITHFUL. I know it very well; it was not the first time that he has met with me. It was he that came to me when I dwelt securely at home, and that told me he would burn my house over my head, if I stayed there.

CHRISTIAN. But did you not see the house that stood there on the top of the hill, on the side of which Moses met you?

FAITHFUL Yes, and the lions too, before I came at it; but for the lions, I think they were asleep; for it was about noon; and because I had so much of the day before me, I passed by the porter, and came down the hill.

CHRISTIAN. He told me indeed, that he saw you go by, but I wish you had called at the house, for they would have showed you so many rarities, that you would scarce have forgot them to the day of your death. But pray tell me, Did you meet nobody in the Valley of Humility?

FAITHFUL. Yes, I met with one Discontent, who would willingly have persuaded me to go back again with him; his reason was, for that the valley was altogether without honour. He told me, moreover, that there to go was the way to disobey all my friends, as Pride, Arrogancy, Self-conceit, Worldly-glory, with others, who, he knew, as he said, would be very much offended, if I made such a fool of myself as to wade through this valley.

CHRISTIAN. Well, and how did you answer him?

FAITHFUL. I told him that although all these that he named might claim kindred of me, and that rightly, for indeed they were my relations according to the flesh, yet since I became a pilgrim, they have disowned me, as I also have rejected them; and therefore they were to me now no more than if they had never been of my lineage.

I told him, moreover, that as to this valley he had quite mis-represented the thing; for before honour is humility; and a haughty spirit before a fall. Therefore, said I, I had rather go through this valley to the honour that was so accounted by the wisest, than chuse that which he esteemed most worthy our affections.

CHRISTIAN. Met you with nothing else in that valley?

FAITHFUL. Yes, I met with Shame; but of all the men that I met with in my pilgrimage, he, I think, bears the wrong name. The others would be said nay, after a little argumentation, and somewhat else; but this bold-faced Shame would never have done.

CHRISTIAN. Why, what did he say to you?

FAITHFUL. What! why, he objected against religion itself; he said it was a pitiful, low, sneaking business for a man to mind religion; he said that a tender conscience was an unmanly thing; and that for a man to watch over his words and ways, so as to tie up himself from that hectoring liberty, that the brave spirits of the times accustom themselves unto, would make him the ridicule of the times. He objected also, that but few of the mighty, rich, or wise, were ever of my opinion; nor any of them neither, before they were persuaded to be fools, and to be of a voluntary fondness, to venture the loss of all, for nobody knows what. He moreover objected the base and low estate and condition of those that were chiefly the pilgrims of the times in which they lived; also their ignorance, and want of understanding in all natural science. Yea, he did hold me to it at that rate also, about a great many more things than here I relate; as, that it was a shame to sit whining and mourning under a sermon, and a shame to come sighing and groaning home; that it was a shame to ask my neighbour forgiveness for petty faults, or to make restitution where I have taken from any. He said also, that religion made a man grow strange to the great, because of a few vices, which he called by finer names; and made him own and respect the base, because of the same religous fraternity. And is not this, said he, a shame?

CHRISTIAN. And what did you say to him?

FAITHFUL. Say! I could not tell what to say at the first. Yea, he put me so to it, that my blood came up in my face; even this Shame fetched it up, and had almost beat me quite off. But, at last, I began to consider, that that which is highly esteemed among men, is had in abomination with God. And I thought again, this Shame tells me what men are; but it tells me nothing what God, or the Word of God is. And I thought, moreover, that at the day of doom, we shall not be doomed to death or life, according to the hectoring spirits of the world, but according to the wisdom and law of the Highest. Therefore, thought I, what God says is best, indeed is best, though all the men in the world are against it. Seeing, then, that God prefers his religion; seeing God prefers a tender conscience; seeing they that make themselves fools for the kingdom of heaven are wisest; and that the poor man that loveth Christ is richer than the greatest man in the world that hates him; Shame, depart, thou art an enemy to my salvation. Shall I entertain thee against my sovereign Lord? How then shall I look him in the face at his coming? Should I now be ashamed of his ways and servants, how can I expect the blessing? But, indeed, this Shame was a bold villain; I could scarce shake him out of my company; yea, he would be haunting of me, and continually whispering me in the ear, with some one or other of the infirmities that attend religion; but at last I told him it was but in vain to attempt further in this business; for those things that he disdained, in those did I see most glory; and so at last I got past this importunate one. And when I had shaken him off, then I began to sing—

The tryals that those men do meet withal,
That are obedient to the heavenly call,
Are manifold, and suited to the flesh,
And come, and come, and come again afresh;

That now, or sometime else, we by them may
Be taken, overcome, and cast away.
O let the pilgrims, let the pilgrims, then,
Be vigilant, and quit themselves like men.

CHRISTIAN. I am glad, my brother, that thou didst withstand this villain so bravely; for of all, as thou sayest, I think he has the wrong name; for he is so bold as to follow us in the streets, and to attempt to put us to shame before all men; that is, to make us ashamed of that which is good; but if he was not himself audacious, he would never attempt to do as he does. But let us still resist him; for notwithstanding all his bravadoes, he promoteth the fool, and none else. The wise shall inherit glory, said Solomon, but shame shall be the promotion of fools.

FAITHFUL. I think we must cry to him for help against Shame, who would have us to be valiant for the truth upon the earth.

CHRISTIAN. You say true; but did you meet nobody else in that valley?

FAITHFUL. No, not I, for I had sun-shine all the rest of the way through that, and also through the Valley of the Shadow of Death.

CHRISTIAN. It was well for you. I am sure it fared far otherwise with me; I had for a long season, as soon almost as I entered into that valley, a dreadful combat with that foul fiend Apollyon; yea, I thought verily he would have killed me, especially when he got me down and crushed me under him, as if he would have crushed me to pieces; for as he threw me, my sword flew out of my hand; nay, he told me he was sure of me; but I cried to God, and he heard me, and delivered me out of all my troubles. Then I entered into the Valley of the Shadow of Death, and had no light for almost half the way through it. I thought I should have been killed there, over and over; but at last day broke, and the sun rose, and I went through that which was behind with far more ease and quiet.

Moreover, I saw in my dream, that as they went on, Faithful, as he chanced to look on one side, saw a man whose name is Talkative, walking at a distance besides them; for in this place, there was room enough for them all to walk. He was a tall man, and something more comely at a distance than at hand. To this man Faithful addressed himself in this manner.

FAITHFUL. Friend, whither away? Are you going to the heavenly country?

TALKATIVE. I am going to the same place.

FAITHFUL. That is well; then I hope we may have your good company.

TALKATIVE. With a very good will, will I be your companion.

FAITHFUL. Come on, then, and let us go together, and let us spend our time in discoursing of things that are profitable.

TALKATIVE. To talk of things that are good, to me is very acceptable, with you, or with any other; and I am glad that I have met with those that incline to so good a work; for, to speak the truth, there are but few that care thus to spend their time (as they are in their travels), but chuse much rather to be speaking of things to no profit; and this hath been a trouble to me.

FAITHFUL. That is indeed a thing to be lamented; for what things so worthy of the use of the tongue and mouth of men on earth, as are the things of the God of heaven?

TALKATIVE. I like you wonderful well, for your sayings are full of conviction; and I will add, what thing is so pleasant, and what so profitable, as to talk of the things of God? What things so pleasant (that is, if a man hath any delight in things that are wonderful)? For instance, if a man doth delight to talk of the history or the mystery of things; or if a man doth love to talk of miracles, wonders, or signs, where shall he find things recorded so delightful, and so sweetly penned, as in the Holy Scripture?

FAITHFUL. That is true; but to be profited by such things in our talk should be that which we design.

TALKATIVE. That is it that I said; for to talk of such things is most profitable; for by so doing, a man may get knowledge of many things; as of vanity of earthly things, and the benefit of things above. Thus, in general, but more particularly, by this, a man may learn the necessity of the new birth; the insufficiency of our works; the need of Christ's righteousness, etc. Besides, by this a man may learn, by talk, what it is to repent, to believe, to pray, to suffer, or the like; by this also a man may learn what are the great promises and consolations of the gospel, to his own comfort. Further, by this a man may learn to refute false opinions, to vindicate the truth, and also to instruct the ignorant.

FAITHFUL. All this is true, and glad am I to hear these things from you.

TALKATIVE. Alas! the want of this is the cause why so few understand the need of faith, and the necessity of a work of grace in their soul, in order to eternal life; but ignorantly live in the works of the law, by which a man can by no means obtain the kingdom of heaven.

FAITHFUL. But, by your leave, heavenly knowledge of these is the gift of God; no man attaineth to them by human industry, or only by the talk of them.

TALKATIVE. All this I know very well. For a man can receive nothing, except it be given him from heaven: all is of grace, not of works. I could give you a hundred scriptures for the confirmation of this.

FAITHFUL. Well, then, said Faithful, what is that one thing that we shall at this time found our discourse upon?

TALKATIVE. What you will. I will talk of things heavenly, or things earthly; things moral, or things evangelical; things sacred, or things profane; things past, or things to come; things foreign, or things at home; things more essential, or things circumstantial; provided that all be done to our profit.

FAITHFUL. Now did Faithful begin to wonder; and stepping to Christian (for he walked all this while by himself), he said to him (but softly), What a brave companion have we got! Surely this man will make a very excellent pilgrim.

CHRISTIAN. At this Christian modestly smiled, and said, This man, with whom you are so taken, will beguile, with that tongue of his, twenty of them that know him not.

FAITHFUL. Do you know him, then?

CHRISTIAN. Know him! Yes, better than he knows himself.

FAITHFUL. Pray, what is he?

CHRISTIAN. His name is Talkative; he dwelleth in our town; I wonder that you should be a stranger to him, only I consider that our town is large.

FAITHFUL. Whose son is he? And whereabouts does he dwell?

CHRISTIAN. He is the son of one Say-well; he dwelt in Prating Row; and he is known of all that are acquainted with him, by the name of Talkative in Prating Row; and notwithstanding his fine tongue, he is but a sorry fellow.

FAITHFUL. Well, he seems to be a very pretty man.

CHRISTIAN. That is, to them who have not thorough acquaintance with him; for he is best abroad; near home, he is ugly enough. Your saying that he is a pretty man, brings to my mind what I have observed in the work of the painter, whose pictures show best at a distance, but, very near, more unpleasing.

FAITHFUL. But I am ready to think you do but jest, because you smiled.

CHRISTIAN. God forbid that I should jest (although I smiled) in this matter, or that I should accuse any falsely! I will give you a further discovery of him. This man is for any company, and for any talk; as he talketh now with you, so will he talk when he is on the ale-bench; and the more drink he hath in his crown, the more of these things he hath in his mouth; religion hath no place in his heart, or house, or conversation; all he hath, lieth in his tongue, and his religion is to make a noise therewith.

FAITHFUL. Say you so! then am I in this man greatly deceived.

CHRISTIAN. Deceived! you may be sure of it; remember the proverb, They say, and do not. But the kingdom of God is not in word, but in power. He talketh of prayer, of repentance, of faith, and of the new birth; but he knows but only to talk of them. I have been in his family, and have observed him both at home and abroad; and I know what I say of him is the truth. His house is as empty of religion, as the white of an egg is of savour. There is there, neither prayer, nor sign of repentance for sin; yea, the brute is his kind serves God far better than he. He is the very stain, reproach, and shame of religion, to all that know him; it can hardly have a good word in all that end of the town where he dwells, through him. Thus say the common people that know him, A saint abroad, and a devil at home. His poor family finds it so, he is such a churl, such a railer at, and so unreasonable with his servants, that they neither know how to do for, or speak to him. Men that have any dealings with him, say, it is better to deal with a Turk than with him; for fairer dealing they shall have at their hands. This Talkative (if it be possible) will go beyond them, defraud, beguile, and over-reach them. Besides, he brings up his sons to follow his steps; and if he findeth in any of them a foolish timorousness (for so he

45

calls the first appearance of a tender conscience), he calls them fools, and blockheads, and by no means will employ them in much, or speak to their commendations before others. For my part, I am of opinion, that he has, by his wicked life, caused many to stumble and fall; and will be, if God prevent not, the ruin of many more.

FAITHFUL. Well, my brother, I am bound to believe you; not only because you say you know him, but also because, like a Christian, you make your reports of men. For I cannot think that you speak these things of ill-will, but because it is even so as you say.

CHRISTIAN. Had I known him no more than you, I might perhaps have thought of him as, at the first, you did; yea, had he received this report at their hands only that are enemies to religion, I should have thought it had been a slander—a lot that often falls from bad men's mouths upon good men's names and professions; but all these things, yea, and a great many more as bad, of my own knowledge, I can prove him guilty of. Besides, good men are ashamed of him; they can neither call him brother, nor friend; the very naming of him among them makes them blush, if they know him.

FAITHFUL. Well, I see that saying and doing are two things, and hereafter I shall better observe this distinction.

CHRISTIAN. They are two things indeed, and are as diverse as are the soul and the body; as the body without the soul is but a dead carcass, so saying, if it be alone, is but a dead carcass also. The soul of religion is the practick part: pure religion and undefiled, before God and the Father, is this, to visit the fatherless and widows in their affliction, and to keep himself unspotted from the world. This Talkative is not aware of; he thinks that hearing and saying will make a good Christian, and thus he deceiveth his own soul. Hearing is but as the sowing of the seed; talking is not sufficient to prove that fruit is indeed in the heart and life; and let us assure ourselves, that at the day of doom men shall be judged according to their fruits. It will not be said then, Did you believe? but, Were you doers, or talkers only? and accordingly shall they be judged. The end of the world is compared to our harvest; and you know men at harvest regard nothing but fruit. Not that anything can be accepted that is not of faith, but I speak this to show you how insignificant the profession of Talkative will be at that day.

FAITHFUL. This brings to my mind that of Moses, by which he describeth the beast that is clean. He is such a one that parteth the hoof and cheweth the cud; not that parteth the hoof only, or that cheweth the cud only. The hare cheweth the cud, but yet is unclean, because he parteth not the hoof. And this truly resembleth Talkative, he cheweth the cud, he seeketh knowledge, he cheweth upon the word; but he divideth not the hoof, he parteth not with the way of sinners; but, as the hare, he retaineth the foot of a dog or bear, and therefore he is unclean.

CHRISTIAN. You have spoken, for aught I know, the true gospel sense of those texts. And I will add another thing: Paul calleth some men, yea, and those great talkers too, sounding brass, and tinkling cymbals, that is, as he expounds them in another place, things without life, giving sound. Things without life, that is, without the true faith and grace of the gospel; and consequently, things that shall never be placed in the kingdom of heaven among those that are the children of life; though their sound, by their talk, be as if it were the tongue or voice of an angel.

FAITHFUL. Well, I was not so fond of his company at first, but I am sick of it now. What shall we do to be rid of him?

CHRISTIAN. Take my advice, and do as I bid you, and you shall find that he will soon be sick of your company too, except God shall touch his heart, and turn it.

FAITHFUL. What would you have me to do?

CHRISTIAN. Why, go to him, and enter into some serious discourse about the power of religion; and ask him plainly (when he has approved of it, for that he will) whether this thing be set up in his heart, house, or conversation?

FAITHFUL. Then Faithful stepped forward again, and said to Talkative, Come, what cheer? How is it now?

TALKATIVE. Thank you, well. I thought we should have had a great deal of talk by this time.

FAITHFUL. Well, if you will, we will fall to it now; and since you left it with me to state the question, let it be this: How doth the saving grace of God discover itself, when it is in the heart of man?

TALKATIVE. I perceive then, that our talk must be about the power of things. Well, it is a very good question, and I shall be willing to answer you. And take my answer in brief, thus: First, Where the grace of God is in the heart, it causeth there a great outcry against sin. Secondly—

FAITHFUL. Nay, hold, let us consider of one at once. I think you should rather say, It shows itself by inclining the soul to abhor its sin.

TALKATIVE. Why, what difference is there between crying out against, and abhorring of sin?

FAITHFUL. O! a great deal. A man may cry out against sin of policy, but he cannot abhor it, but by virtue of a godly antipathy against it. I have heard many cry out against sin in the pulpit, who yet can abide it well enough in the heart, house, and conversation. Some cry out against sin, even as the mother cries out against her child in her lap, when she calleth it slut and naughty girl, and then falls to hugging and kissing it.

TALKATIVE. You lie at the catch, I perceive.

FAITHFUL. No, not I; I am only for setting things right. But what is the second thing whereby you would prove a discovery of a work of grace in the heart?

TALKATIVE. Great knowledge of gospel mysteries.

FAITHFUL. This sign should have been first; but first or last, it is also false; for knowledge, great knowledge, may be obtained in the mysteries of the gospel, and yet no work of grace in the soul. Yea, if a man have all knowledge, he may yet be nothing, and so consequently be no child of God. When Christ said, Do you know all these things? and the disciples had answered, Yes; he addeth, Blessed are ye if ye do them. He doth not lay the blessing in the knowing of them, but in the doing of them. For there is a knowledge that is not attended with doing: He that knoweth his master's will, and doeth it not. A man may know like an angel, and yet be no Christian, therefore your sign of it is not true. Indeed, to know is a thing that pleaseth talkers and boasters; but to do is that which pleaseth God. Not that the heart can be good without knowledge; for without that the heart is naught. There is, therefore, knowledge and knowledge. Knowledge that resteth in the bare speculation of things; and knowledge that is accompanied with the grace of faith and love; which puts a man upon doing even the will of God from the heart: the first of these will serve the talker; but without the other the true Christian is not content. Give me understanding, and I shall keep thy law; yea, I shall observe it with my whole heart.

TALKATIVE. You lie at the catch again; this is not for edification.

FAITHFUL. Well, if you please, propound another sign how this work of grace discovereth itself where it is.

TALKATIVE. Not I, for I see we shall not agree.

FAITHFUL. Well, if you will not, will you give me leave to do it?

TALKATIVE. You may use your liberty.

FAITHFUL. A work of grace in the soul discovereth itself, either to him that hath it, or to standers by.

To him that hath it thus: It gives him conviction of sin, especially of the defilement of his nature and the sin of unbelief (for the sake of which he is sure to be damned, if he findeth not mercy at God's hand, by faith in Jesus Christ). This sight and sense of things worketh in him sorrow and shame for sin; he findeth, moreover, revealed in him the Saviour of the world, and the absolute necessity of closing with him for life, at the which he findeth hungerings and thirstings after him; to which hungerings, etc., the promise is made. Now, according to the strength or weakness of his faith in his Saviour, so is his joy and peace, so is his love to holiness, so are his desires to know him more, and also to serve him in this world. But though I say it discovereth itself thus unto him, yet it is but seldom that he is able to conclude that this is a work of grace; because his corruptions now, and his abused reason, make his mind to misjudge in this matter; therefore, in him that hath this work, there is required a very sound judgment before he can, with steadiness, conclude that this is a work of grace.

To others, it is thus discovered:

1. By an experimental confession of his faith in Christ.

2. By a life answerable to that confession; to wit, a life of holiness; heart-holiness; family-holiness (if he hath a family), and by conversation-holiness in the world; which, in the general, teacheth him, inwardly, to abhor his sin, and himself for that, in secret; to suppress it in his family, and to promote holiness in the world; not by talk only, as a hypocrite or talkative person may do, but by a practical subjection, in faith and love, to

48

the power of the Word. And now, Sir, as to this brief description of the work of grace, and also the discovery of it, if you have aught to object, object; if not, then give me leave to propound to you a second question.

TALKATIVE. Nay, my part is not now to object, but to hear; let me, therefore, have your second question.

FAITHFUL. It is this: Do you experience this first part of this description of it? and doth your life and conversation testify the same? or standeth your religion in word or in tongue, and not in deed and truth? Pray, if you incline to answer me in this, say no more than you know the God above will say Amen to; and, also, nothing but what your conscience can justify you in; for, not he that commendeth himself is approved, but whom the Lord commendeth. Besides, to say, I am thus, and thus, when my conversation, and all my neighbours, tell me I lie, is great wickedness.

TALKATIVE. Then Talkative at first began to blush; but, recovering himself, thus he replied: You come now to experience, to conscience, and God; and to appeal to him for justification of what is spoken. This kind of discourse I did not expect; nor am I disposed to give an answer to such questions, because I count not myself bound thereto, unless you take upon you to be a catechizer, and, though you should so do, yet I may refuse to make you my judge. But, I pray, tell me why you ask me such questions?

FAITHFUL. Because I saw you forward to talk, and because I knew not that you had aught else but notion. Besides, to tell you all the truth, I have heard of you, that you are a man whose religion lies in talk, and that your conversation gives this your mouth-profession the lie. They say, you are a spot among Christians; and that religion fareth the worse for your ungodly conversation; that some already have stumbled at your wicked ways, and that more are in danger of being destroyed thereby; your religion, and an ale-house, and covetousness, and uncleanness, and swearing, and lying, and vain company keeping, etc., will stand together.

TALKATIVE. Since you are ready to take up reports, and to judge so rashly as you do, I cannot but conclude you are some peevish or melancholy man, not fit to be discoursed with; and so adieu.

CHRISTIAN. Then came up Christian, and said to his brother, I told you how it would happen; your words and his lusts could not agree; he had rather leave your company than reform his life. But he is gone, as I said; let him go, the loss is no man's but his own; he has saved us the trouble of going from him; for he continuing (as I suppose he will do) as he is, he would have been but a blot in our company; besides, the apostle says, From such withdraw thyself.

FAITHFUL. But I am glad we had this little discourse with him; it may happen that he will think of it again; however, I have dealt plainly with him, and so am clear of his blood, if he perisheth.

CHRISTIAN. You did well to talk so plainly to him as you did; there is but little of this faithful dealing with men now-a-days, and that makes religion to stink so in the nostrils of many, as it doth; for they are these talkative fools whose religion is only in word, and are debauched and vain in their conversation, that (being so much admitted into the fellowship of the godly) do puzzle the world, blemish Christianity, and grieve the sincere. I wish that all men would deal with such as you have done; then should they either be made more conformable to religion, or the company of saints would be too hot for them. Then did Faithful say:

How Talkative at first lifts up his plumes!
How bravely doth he speak! How he presumes
To drive down all before him! But so soon
As Faithful talks of heart-work, like the moon
That's past the full, into the wane he goes.
And so will all, but he that heart-work knows.

Thus they went on talking of what they had seen by the way, and so made that way easy which would, otherwise, no doubt, have been tedious to them; for now they went through a wilderness.

Now, when they were got almost quite out of this wilderness, Faithful chanced to cast his eye back, and espied one coming after them, and he knew him. Oh! said Faithful to his brother, Who comes yonder? Then Christian looked, and said, It is my good friend Evangelist. Aye, and my good friend too, said Faithful, for it was he that set me the way to the gate. Now was Evangelist come up unto them, and thus saluted them:

EVANGELIST. Peace be with you, dearly beloved; and peace be to your helpers.

CHRISTIAN. Welcome, welcome, my good Evangelist; the sight of thy countenance brings to my remembrance thy ancient kindness and unwearied labouring for my eternal good.

FAITHFUL. And a thousand times welcome, said good Faithful. Thy company, O sweet Evangelist, how desirable it is to us poor pilgrims!

EVANGELIST. Then said Evangelist, How hath it fared with you, my friends, since the time of our last parting? What have you met with, and how have you behaved yourselves?

Then Christian and Faithful told him of all things that had happened to them in the way; and how, and with what difficulty, they had arrived to that place.

EVANGELIST. Right glad am I, said Evangelist, not that you have met with trials, but that you have been victors; and for that you have, notwithstanding many weaknesses, continued in the way to this very day.

I say, right glad am I of this thing, and that for mine own sake and yours. I have sowed, and you have reaped; and the day is coming, when both he that sowed and they that reaped shall rejoice together; that is, if you hold out; for in due season ye shall reap, if ye faint not. The crown is before you, and it is an incorruptible one; so run, that you may obtain it. Some there be that set out for this crown, and, after they have gone far for it, another comes in, and takes it from them; hold fast, therefore, that you have, let no man take your crown. You are not yet out of the gun-shot of the devil; you have not resisted unto blood, striving against sin; let the kingdom be always before you, and believe steadfastly concerning things that are invisible. Let nothing that is on this side the other world get within you; and, above all, look well to your own hearts, and to the lusts thereof, for they are deceitful above all things, and desperately wicked; set your faces like a flint; you have all power in heaven and earth on your side.

CHRISTIAN. Then Christian thanked him for his exhortation; but told him, withal, that they would have him speak further to them for their help the rest of the way, and the rather, for that they well knew that he was a prophet, and could tell them of things that might happen unto them, and also how they might resist and overcome them. To which request Faithful also consented. So Evangelist began as followeth:

EVANGELIST. My sons, you have heard in the words of the truth of the gospel that you must, through many tribulations, enter into the kingdom of heaven. And again, that in every city bonds and afflictions abide in you; and therefore you cannot expect that you should go long on your pilgrimage without them, in some sort or other. You have found something of the truth of these testimonies upon you already, and more will immediately follow; for now, as you see, you are almost out of this wilderness, and therefore you will soon come into a town that you will by and by see before you; and in that town you will be hardly beset with enemies, who will strain hard but they will kill you; and be you sure that one or both of you must seal the testimony which you hold, with blood; but be you faithful unto death, and the King will give you a crown of life. He that shall die there, although his death will be unnatural, and his pain perhaps great, he will yet have the better of his fellow; not only because he will be arrived at the Celestial City soonest, but because he will escape many miseries that the other will meet with in the rest of his journey. But when you are come to the town, and shall find fulfilled what I have here related, then remember your friend and quit yourselves like men, and commit the keeping of your souls to your God in well-doing, as unto a faithful Creator.

Then I saw in my dream, that when they were got out of the wilderness, they presently saw a town before them, and the name of that town is Vanity; and at the town there is a fair kept, called Vanity Fair: it is kept all the year long; it beareth the name of Vanity Fair, because the town where it is kept is lighter than vanity; and also because all that is there sold, or that cometh thither, is vanity. As is the saying of the wise, All that cometh is vanity.

This fair is no new-erected business, but a thing of ancient standing; I will show you the original of it.

Almost five thousand years agone, there were pilgrims walking to the Celestial City as these two honest persons are: and Beelzebub, Apollyon, and Legion, with their companions, perceiving by the path that the pilgrims made, that their way to the city lay through this town of Vanity, they contrived here to set up a fair; a fair wherein should be sold all sorts of vanity, and that it should last all the year long: therefore at this fair are all such merchandise sold, as houses, lands, trades, places, honours, preferments, titles, countries, kingdoms, lusts, pleasures, and delights of all sorts, as wives, husbands, children, masters, servants, lives, blood, bodies, souls, silver, gold, pearls, precious stones, and what not.

And, moreover, at this fair there is at all times to be seen juggling, cheats, games, plays, fools, apes, knaves, and rogues, and that of every kind.

Here are to be seen too, and that for nothing, thefts, murders, adulteries, false swearers, and that of a blood-red colour.

And as in other fairs of less moment, there are the several rows and streets, under their proper names, where such and such wares are vended; so here likewise you have the proper places, rows, streets (viz. countries and kingdoms), where the wares of this fair are soonest to be found. Here is the Britain Row, the French Row, the Italian Row, the Spanish Row, the German Row, where several sorts of vanities are to be sold. But, as in other fairs, some one commodity is as the chief of all the fair, so the ware of Rome and her merchandise is greatly promoted in this fair; only our English nation, with some others, have taken a dislike thereat.

Now, as I said, the way to the Celestial City lies just through this town where this lusty fair is kept; and he that will go to the City, and yet not go through this town, must needs go out of the world. The Prince of princes himself, when here, went through this town to his own country, and that upon a fair day too; yea, and as I think, it was Beelzebub, the chief lord of this fair, that invited him to buy of his vanities; yea, would have made him lord of the fair, would he but have done him reverence as he went through the town. Yea, because he was such a person of honour, Beelzebub had him from street to street, and showed him all the kingdoms of the world in a little time, that he might, if possible, allure the Blessed One to cheapen and buy some of his vanities; but he had no mind to the merchandise, and therefore left the town, without laying out so much as one farthing upon these vanities. This fair, therefore, is an ancient thing, of long standing, and a very great fair. Now these Pilgrims, as I said, must needs go through this fair. Well, so they did; but, behold, even as they entered into the fair, all the people in the fair were moved, and the town itself as it were in a hubbub about them; and that for several reasons; for—

First, the pilgrims were clothed with such kind of raiment as was diverse from the raiment of any that traded in that fair. The people, therefore, of the fair, made a great gazing upon them: some said they were fools, some they were bedlams, and some they are outlandish men.

Secondly, and as they wondered at their apparel, so they did likewise at their speech; for few could understand what they said; they naturally spoke the language of Canaan, but they that kept the fair were the men of this world; so that, from one end of the fair to the other, they seemed barbarians each to the other.

Thirdly, but that which did not a little amuse the merchandisers was, that these pilgrims set very light by all their wares; they cared not so much as to look upon them; and if they called upon them to buy, they would put their fingers in their ears, and cry, Turn away mine eyes from beholding vanity, and look upwards, signifying that their trade and traffic was in heaven.

One chanced mockingly, beholding the carriage of the men, to say unto them, What will ye buy? But they, looking gravely upon him, answered, We buy the truth. At that there was an occasion taken to despise the men the more: some mocking, some taunting, some speaking reproachfully, and some calling upon others to smite them. At last things came to a hubbub, and great stir in the fair, insomuch that all order was confounded. Now was word presently brought to the great one of the fair, who quickly came down, and deputed some of his most trusty friends to take these men into examination, about whom the fair was almost overturned. So the men were brought to examination; and they that sat upon them, asked them whence they came, whither they went, and what they did there in such an unusual garb? The men told them, that they were pilgrims and strangers in the world, and that they were going to their own country, which was the heavenly Jerusalem; and that they had given no occasion to the men of the town, nor yet to the merchandisers, thus to abuse them, and to let them in their journey, except it was, for that, when one asked them what they would buy, they said would buy the truth. But they that were appointed to examine them did not believe them to be any other than bedlams and mad, or else such as came to put all things into a confusion in the fair. Therefore they took them and beat them, and besmeared them with dirt, and then put them into the cage, that they might be made a spectacle to all the men of the fair. There, therefore, they lay for some time, and were made the objects of any man's sport, or malice, or revenge, the great one of the fair laughing still at all that befell them. But the men being patient, and not rendering railing for railing, but contrariwise, blessing, and giving good words for bad, and kindness for injuries done, some men in the fair that were more observing, and less prejudiced than the rest, began to check and blame the baser sort for their continual abuses done by them to the men; they, therefore, in angry manner, let fly at them again, counting them as bad as the men in the cage, and telling them that they seemed confederates, and should be made partakers of their misfortunes. The other replied, that for aught they could see, the men were quiet, and sober, and intended nobody any harm; and that there were many that traded in their fair, that were more worthy to be put into the cage, yea, and pillory too, than were the men that they had abused. Thus, after divers words had passed on both sides, the men behaving themselves all the while very wisely and soberly before them, they fell to some blows among themselves, and did harm one to another. Then were these two poor men brought before their examiners again, and there charged as being guilty of the late hubbub that had been in the fair. So they beat them pitifully, and hanged irons upon them, and led them in chains up and down the fair, for an example and a terror to others, lest any should speak in their behalf, or join themselves unto them.

But Christian and Faithful behaved themselves yet more wisely, and received the ignominy and shame that was cast upon them, with so much meekness and patience, that it won to their side, though but few in comparison of the rest, several of the men in the fair. This put the other party yet into greater rage, insomuch that they concluded the death of these two men. Wherefore they threatened, that the cage nor irons should serve their turn, but that they should die, for the abuse they had done, and for deluding the men of the fair.

Then were they remanded to the cage again, until further order should be taken with them. So they put them in, and made fast their feet in the stocks.

Here, therefore, they called again to mind what they had heard from their faithful friend Evangelist, and were the more confirmed in their way and sufferings, by what he told them would happen to them. They also now comforted each other, that whose lot it was to suffer, even he should have the best of it; therefore each man secretly wished that he might have that preferment: but committing themselves to the all-wise disposal of Him that ruleth all things, with much content they abode in the condition in which they were, until they should be otherwise disposed of.

Then a convenient time being appointed, they brought them forth to their trial, in order to their condemnation. When the time was come, they were brought before their enemies and arraigned. The Judge's name was Lord Hategood. Their indictment was one and the same in substance, though somewhat varying in form, the contents whereof were this:

That they were enemies to, and disturbers of their trade; that they had made commotions and divisions in the town, and had won a party to their own most dangerous opinions, in contempt of the law of their prince.

Then Faithful began to answer, that he had only set himself against that which had set itself against Him that is higher than the highest. And, said he, as for disturbance, I make none, being myself a man of peace; the parties that were won to us, were won by beholding our truth and innocence, and they are only turned from the worse to the better. And as to the king you talk of, since he is Beelzebub, the enemy of our Lord, I defy him and all his angels.

Then proclamation was made, that they that had aught to say for their lord the king against the prisoner at the bar, should forthwith appear and give in their evidence. So there came in three witnesses, to wit, Envy, Superstition, and Pickthank. They were then asked if they knew the prisoner at the bar; and what they had to say for their lord the king against him.

Then stood forth Envy, and said to this effect: My Lord, I have known this man a long time, and will attest upon my oath before this honourable bench, that he is——

JUDGE. Hold. Give him his oath. (So they sware him.) Then he said——

ENVY. My Lord, this man, notwithstanding his plausible name, is one of the vilest men in our country. He neither regardeth prince nor people, law

54

nor custom; but doth all that he can to possess all men with certain of his disloyal notions, which he in the general calls principles of faith and holiness. And, in particular, I heard him once myself affirm, that Christianity and the customs of our town of Vanity, were diametrically opposite, and could not be reconciled. By which saying, my Lord, he doth at once not only condemn all our laudable doings, but us in the doing of them.

JUDGE. Then did the Judge say to him, Hast thou any more to say?

ENVY. My Lord, I could say much more, only I would not be tedious to the court. Yet, if need be, when the other gentlemen have given in their evidence, rather than anything shall be wanting that will despatch him, I will enlarge my testimony against him. So he was bid stand by.

Then they called Superstition, and bid him look upon the prisoner. They also asked, what he could say for their lord the king against him. Then they sware him; so he began.

SUPERSTITION. My Lord, I have no great acquaintance with this man, nor do I desire to have further knowledge of him; however, this I know, that he is a very pestilent fellow, from some discourse that, the other day, I had with him in this town; for then talking with him, I heard him say, that our religion was naught, and such by which a man could by no means please God. Which saying of his, my Lord, your Lordship very well knows, what necessarily thence will follow, to wit, that we do still worship in vain, are yet in our sins, and finally shall be damned; and this is that which I have to say.

Then was Pickthank sworn, and bid say what he knew, in behalf of their lord the king, against the prisoner at the bar.

PICKTHANK. My Lord, and you gentleman all, This fellow I have known of a long time, and have heard him speak things that ought not to be spoke; for he hath railed on our noble prince Beelzebub, and hath spoken contemptibly of his honourable friends, whose names are the Lord Old Man, the Lord Carnal Delight, the Lord Luxurious, the Lord Desire of Vain Glory, my old Lord Lechery, Sir Having Greedy, with all the rest of our nobility; and he hath said, moreover, That if all men were of his mind, if possible, there is not one of these noblemen should have any longer a being in this town. Besides, he hath not been afraid to rail on you, my Lord, who are now appointed to be his judge, calling you an ungodly villain, with many other such like vilifying terms, with which he hath bespattered most of the gentry of our town.

When this Pickthank had told his tale, the Judge directed his speech to the prisoner at the bar, saying, Thou runagate, heretic, and traitor, hast thou heard what these honest gentlemen have witnessed against thee?

FAITHFUL. May I speak a few words in my own defence?

JUDGE. Sirrah! Sirrah! thou deservest to live no longer, but to be slain immediately upon the place; yet, that all men may see our gentleness towards thee, let us see what thou, vile runagate, hast to say.

FAITHFUL. 1. I say, then, in answer to what Mr. Envy hath spoken, I never said aught but this, That what rule, or laws, or custom, or people, were flat against the Word of God, are diametrically opposite to Christianity. If I have said amiss in this, convince me of my error, and I am ready here before you to make my recantation.

2. As to the second, to wit, Mr. Superstition, and his charge against me, I said only this, That in the worship of God there is required a Divine faith; but there can be no Divine faith without a Divine revelation of the will of God. Therefore, whatever is thrust into the worship of God that is not agreeable to Divine revelation, cannot be done but by a human faith, which faith will not be profitable to eternal life.

3. As to what Mr. Pickthank hath said, I say (avoiding terms, as that I am said to rail, and the like), that the prince of this town, with all the rabblement, his attendants, by this gentleman named, are more fit for a being in hell, than in this town and country: and so, the Lord have mercy upon me!

Then the Judge called to the jury (who all this while stood by, to hear and observe); Gentlemen of the jury, you see this man about whom so great an uproar hath been made in this town. You have also heard what these worthy gentlemen have witnessed against him. Also you have heard his reply and confession. It lieth now in your breasts to hang him, or save his life; but yet I think meet to instruct you into our law.

There was an Act made in the days of Pharaoh the Great, servant to our prince, that lest those of a contrary religion should multiply, and grow too strong for him, their males should be thrown into the river. There was also an Act made in the days of Nebuchadnezzar the Great, another of his servants, that whosoever would not fall down and worship his golden image, should be thrown into a fiery furnace. There was also an Act made in the days of Darius, that whoso, for some time, called upon any God but him, should be cast into the lions' den. Now the substance of these laws this rebel has broken, not only in thought (which is not to be borne) but also in word and deed; which must therefore needs be intolerable.

For that of Pharaoh, his law was made upon a supposition, to prevent mischief, no crime being yet apparent; but here is a crime apparent. For the second and third, you see he disputeth against our religion; and for the treason he hath confessed, he deserveth to die the death.

Then went the jury out, whose nomes were, Mr. Blindman, Mr. No-good, Mr. Malice, Mr. Love-lust, Mr. Live-loose, Mr. Heady, Mr. High-mind, Mr. Enmity, Mr. Lyar, Mr. Cruelty, Mr. Hate-light, and Mr. Implacable; who every one gave in his private verdict against him among themselves, and afterwards unanimously concluded to bring him in guilty before the Judge. And first, among themselves, Mr. Blindman, the foreman, said, I see clearly that this man is a heretic. Then said Mr. No-good, Away with such a fellow from the earth. Ay, said Mr. Malice, for I hate the very looks of him. Then said Mr. Love-lust, I could never endure him. Nor I, said Mr. Live-loose, for he would always be condemning my way. Hang him, hang him, said Mr. Heady. A sorry scrub, said Mr. High-mind. My heart riseth against him, said Mr. Enmity. He is a rogue, said Mr. Lyar. Hanging is too good for him, said Mr. Cruelty. Let us despatch him out of the way, said Mr. Hate-light. Then said Mr. Implacable, Might I have all the world given me, I could not be reconciled to him; therefore, let us forthwith bring him in guilty of death. And so they did; therefore he was presently condemned, to be had from the place where he was, to the place from whence he came, and there to be put to the most cruel death that could be invented.

They, therefore, brought him out, to do with him according to their law; and, first, they scourged him, then they buffeted him, then they lanced his flesh with knives; after that, they stoned him with stones, then pricked him with their swords; and, last of all, they burned him to ashes at the stake. Thus came Faithful to his end.

Now I saw that there stood behind the multitude, a chariot and a couple of horses, waiting for Faithful, who (so soon as his adversaries had despatched him) was taken up into it, and straightway was carried up through the clouds, with sound of trumpet, the nearest way to the Celestial Gate.

But as for Christian, he had some respite, and was remanded back to prison. So he there remained for a space; but he that overrules all things, having the power of their rage in his own hand, so wrought it about, that Christian for that time escaped them, and went his way; and as he went, he sang, saying:

> Well, Faithful, thou hast faithfully profest
> Unto thy Lord; with whom thou shalt be blest,
> When faithless ones, with all their vain delights,
> Are crying out under their hellish plights.
> Sing, Faithful, sing, and let thy name survive;
> For, though they kill'd thee, thou art yet alive.

Now I saw in my dream, that Christian went not forth alone, for there was one whose name was Hopeful (being made so by the beholding of Christian and Faithful in their words and behaviour, in their sufferings at the Fair), who joined himself unto him, and, entering into a brotherly covenant, told him that he would be his companion. Thus, one died to bear testimony to the truth, and another rises out of his ashes, to be a companion with Christian in his pilgrimage.

They went then till they came to the Delectable Mountains, which mountains belong to the Lord of that hill of which we have spoken before; so they went up to the mountains, to behold the gardens and orchards, the vineyards and fountains of water; where also they drank and washed themselves, and did freely eat of the vineyards. Now there were on the tops of these mountains, shepherds feeding their flocks, and they stood by the highway side. The Pilgrims therefore went to them, and leaning upon their staves (as is common with weary pilgrims, when they stand to talk with any by the way), they asked, Whose Delectable Mountains are these? And whose be the sheep that feed upon them?

SHEPHERDS. These mountains are Immanuel's Land, and they are within sight of his city; and the sheep also are his, and he laid down his life for them.

CHRISTIAN. Is this the way to the Celestial City?

SHEPHERDS. You are just in your way.

CHRISTIAN. How far is it thither?

SHEPHERDS. Too far for any but those that shall get thither indeed.

CHRISTIAN. Is the way safe or dangerous?

SHEPHERDS. Safe for those for whom it is to be safe; but the transgressors shall fall therein.

CHRISTIAN. Is there, in this place, any relief for pilgrims that are weary and faint in the way?

SHEPHERDS. The Lord of these mountains hath given us a charge not to be forgetful to entertain strangers; therefore the good of the place is before you.

I saw also in my dream, that when the Shepherds perceived that they were wayfaring men, they also put questions to them, to which they made answer as in other places; as, Whence came you? And, How go you into the way? And, By what means have you so persevered therein? For but few of them that begin to come hither, do show their face on these mountains. But when the Shepherds heard their answers, being pleased therewith, they looked very lovingly upon them, and said, Welcome to the Delectable Mountains.

The Shepherds, I say, whose names were Knowledge, Experience, Watchful, and Sincere, took them by the hand, and had them to their tents, and made them partake of that which was ready at present. They said, moreover, We would that ye should stay here a while, to be acquainted with us; and yet more to solace yourselves with the good of these Delectable Mountains. They then told them that they were content to stay; so they went to their rest that night because it was very late.

Then I saw in my dream, that in the morning the Shepherds called up Christian and Hopeful to walk with them upon the mountains: so they went forth with them, and walked a while, having a pleasant prospect on every side. Then said the Shepherds one to another, Shall we show these Pilgrims some wonders? So when they had concluded to do it, they had them first to the top of a hill called Error, which was very steep on the farthest side, and bid them look down to the bottom. So Christian and Hopeful looked down, and saw at the bottom several men dashed all to pieces by a fall that they had from the top. Then said Christian, What meaneth this? The Shepherds answered, Have you not heard of them that were made to err, by hearkening to Hymeneus and Philetus, as concerning the faith of resurrection of the body? They answered, Yes. Then said the Shepherds, Those that you see lie dashed in pieces at the bottom of this mountain are they; and they have continued to this day unburied, as you see, for an example to others to take heed how they clamber too high, or how they come too near the brink of this mountain.

Then I saw that they had them to the top of another mountain, and the name of that is Caution, and bid them look afar off; which, when they did, they perceived, as they thought, several men walking up and down among the tombs that were there; and they perceived that the men were blind, because they stumbled sometimes upon the tombs, and because they could not get out from among them. Then said Christian, What means this?

The Shepherds then answered, Did you not see a little below these mountains a stile that led into a meadow, on the left hand of this way? They answered, Yes. Then said the Shepherds, From that there goes a path that leads directly to Doubting Castle, which is kept by Giant Despair, and these, pointing to them among the tombs, came once on pilgrimage as you do now, even till they came to that same stile; and because the right way was rough in that place, they chose to go out of it into that meadow, and there were taken by Giant Despair, and cast into Doubting Castle: where, after they had been a while kept in the dungeon, he at last did put out their eyes, and led them among those tombs, where he has left them to wander to this very day, that the saying of the wise man might be fulfilled, He that wandereth out of the way of understanding, shall remain in the congregation of the dead. Then Christian and Hopeful looked upon one another, with tears gushing out, but yet said nothing to the Shepherds.

Then I saw in my dream, that the Shepherds had them to another place, in a bottom, where was a door in the side of a hill, and they opened the door, and bid them look in. They looked in, therefore, and saw that within it was very dark and smoky; they also thought that they heard a rumbling noise as of fire, and a cry of some tormented, and that they smelt the scent of brimstone. Then said Christian, What means this? The Shepherds told them, This is a by-way to hell, a way that hypocrites go in at; namely, such as sell their birthright, with Esau; such as sell their master, with Judas; such as blaspheme the gospel, with Alexander; and that lie and dissemble, with Ananias and Sapphira his wife. Then said Hopeful to the Shepherds, I perceive that these had on them, even every one, a show of pilgrimage, as we have now; had they not?

SHEPHERDS. Yes, and held it a long time too.

HOPEFUL. How far might they go on in pilgrimage in their day, since they notwithstanding were thus miserably cast away?

SHEPHERDS. Some further, and some not so far as these mountains.

Then said the Pilgrims one to another, We had need to cry to the Strong for strength.

SHEPHERDS. Aye, and you will have need to use it, when you have it, too.

By this time the Pilgrims had a desire to go forward, and the Shepherds a desire they should; so they walked together towards the end of the mountains. Then said the Shepherds to one another, Let us here show to the Pilgrims the gates of the Celestial City, if they have skill to look through our perspective glass. The Pilgrims then lovingly accepted the motion; so they had them to the top of a high hill, called Clear, and gave them their glass to look.

Then they essayed to look, but the remembrance of that last thing that the Shepherds had showed them, made their hands shake; by means of which impediment, they could not look steadily through the glass; yet they thought they saw something like the gate, and also some of the glory of the place. Then they went away, and sang this song:

> Thus, by the Shepherds, secrets are reveal'd,
> Which from all other men are kept conceal'd.
> Come to the Shepherds, then, if you would see
> Things deep, things hid, and that mysterious be.

When they were about to depart, one of the Shepherds gave them a note of the way. Another of them bid them beware of the Flatterer. The third bid them take heed that they sleep not upon the Inchanted Ground. And the fourth bid them God speed. So I awoke from my dream.

And I slept, and dreamed again, and saw the same two Pilgrims going down the mountains along the highway towards the city. Now, a little below these mountains, on the left hand, lieth the country of Conceit; from which country there comes into the way in which the Pilgrims walked, a little crooked lane. Here, therefore, they met with a very brisk lad, that came out of that country; and his name was Ignorance. So Christian asked him from what parts he came, and whither he was going.

IGNORANCE. Sir, I was born in the country that lieth off there, a little on the left hand, and I am going to the Celestial City.

CHRISTIAN. But how do you think to get in at the gate? for you may find some difficulty there.

IGNORANCE. As other good people do, said he.

CHRISTIAN. But what have you to show at that gate, that may cause that the gate should be opened to you?

IGNORANCE. I know my Lord's will, and I have been a good liver; I pray every man his own; I pray, fast, pay tithes, and give alms, and have left my country for whither I am going.

CHRISTIAN. But thou camest not in at the wicket-gate that is at the head of this way; thou camest in hither through that same crooked lane, and therefore, I fear, however thou mayest think of thyself, when the reckoning day shall come, thou wilt have laid to thy charge that thou art a thief and a robber, instead of getting admittance into the city.

IGNORANCE. Gentlemen, ye be utter strangers to me, I know you not; be content to follow the religion of your country, and I will follow the religion of mine. I hope all will be well. And as for the gate that you talk of, all the world knows that that is a great way off of our country. I cannot think that any man in all our parts doth so much as know the way to it, nor need they matter whether they do or no, since we have, as you see, a fine pleasant green lane, that comes down from our country, the next way into the way.

When Christian saw that the man was wise in his own conceit, he said to Hopeful, whisperingly, There is more hope of a fool than of him. And said, moreover, When he that is a fool walketh by the way, his wisdom faileth him, and he saith to every one that he is a fool. What, shall we talk further with him, or outgo him at present, and so leave him to think of what he hath heard already, and then stop again for him afterwards, and see if by degrees we can do any good to him? Then said Hopeful:

Let Ignorance a little while now muse
On what is said, and let him not refuse
Good counsel to embrace, lest he remain
Still ignorant of what's the chiefest gain.
God saith, those that no understanding have,
Although he made them, them he will not save.

HOPEFUL. He further added, It is not good, I think, to say all to him at once; let us pass him by, if you will, and talk to him anon, even as he is able to bear it.

So they both went on, and Ignorance he came after. Now when they had passed him a little way, they entered into a very dark lane, where they met a man whom seven devils had bound with seven strong cords, and were carrying of him back to the door that they saw on the side of the hill. Now good Christian began to tremble, and so did Hopeful his companion; yet as the devils led away the man, Christian looked to see if he knew him; and he thought it might be one Turn-away, that dwelt in the town of Apostasy. But he did not perfectly see his face, for he did hang his head like a thief that is found. But being once past, Hopeful looked after him, and espied on his back a paper with this inscription, Wanton professor, and damnable apostate. Then said Christian to his fellow, Now I call to remembrance, that which was told me of a thing that happened to a good man hereabout. The name of the man was Little-faith, but a good man, and he dwelt in the town of Sincere. The thing was this: At the entering in at this passage, there comes down from Broad-way Gate, a lane called Dead Man's Lane; so called because of the murders that are commonly done there; and this Little-faith going on pilgrimage, as we do now, chanced to sit down there, and slept. Now there happened, at that time, to come down the lane from Broad-way Gate, three sturdy rogues, and their names were Faint-heart, Mistrust, and Guilt (three brothers), and they espying Little-faith, where he was, came galloping up with speed. Now the good man was just awake from his sleep, and was getting up to go on his journey. So they came up all to him, and with threatening language bid him stand. At this, Little-faith looked as white as a clout, and had neither power to fight nor fly. Then said Faint-heart, Deliver thy purse. But he making no haste to do it (for he was loath to lose his money), Mistrust ran up to him, and thrusting his hand into his pocket, pulled out thence a bag of silver. Then he cried out, Thieves! Thieves! With that, Guilt, with a great club that was in his hand, struck Little-faith on the head, and with that blow felled him flat on the ground; where he lay bleeding as one that would bleed to death. All this while the thieves stood by. But, at last, they hearing that some were upon the road, and fearing lest it should be one Great-grace, that dwells in the city of Good-confidence, they betook themselves to their heels, and left this good man to shift for himself. Now, after a while, Little-faith came to himself, and getting up, made shift to scrabble on his way. This was the story.

HOPEFUL. But did they take from him all that ever he had?

CHRISTIAN. No; the place where his jewels were they never ransacked, so those he kept still. But, as I was told, the good man was much afflicted for his loss, for the thieves got most of his spending-money. That which they got not (as I said) were jewels, also he had a little odd money left, but scarce enough to bring him to his journey's end; nay, if I was not misinformed, he was forced to beg as he went, to keep himself alive; for his jewels he might not sell. But beg, and do what he could, he went (as we say) with many a hungry belly the most part of the rest of the way.

HOPEFUL. But is it not a wonder they got not from him his certificate, by which he was to receive his admittance at the Celestial Gate?

CHRISTIAN. It is a wonder; but they got not that, though they missed it not through any good cunning of his; for he, being dismayed with their coming upon him, had neither power nor skill to hide anything; so it was more by good Providence than by his endeavour, that they missed of that good thing.

HOPEFUL. But it must needs be a comfort to him, that they got not this jewel from him.

CHRISTIAN. It might have been great comfort to him, had he used it as he should; but they that told me the story said, that he made but little use of it all the rest of the way, and that because of the dismay that he had in their taking away his money; indeed, he forgot it a great part of the rest of his journey; and besides, when at any time it came into his mind, and he began to be comforted therewith, then would fresh thoughts of his loss come again upon him, and those thoughts would swallow up all.

HOPEFUL. Alas! poor man. This could not but be a great grief to him.

CHRISTIAN. Grief! aye, a grief indeed. Would it not have been so to any of us, had we been used as he, to be robbed, and wounded too, and that in a strange place, as he was? It is a wonder he did not die with grief, poor heart! I was told that he scattered almost all the rest of the way with nothing but doleful and bitter complaints; telling also to all that overtook him. or that he overtook in the way as he went, where he was robbed, and how; who they were that did it, and what he lost; how he was wounded, and that he hardly escaped with his life.

HOPEFUL. But it is a wonder that his necessity did not put him upon selling or pawning some of his jewels, that he might have wherewith to relieve himself in his journey.

CHRISTIAN. Thou talkest like one upon whose head is the shell to this very day; for what should he pawn them, or to whom should he sell them? In all that country where he was robbed, his jewels were not accounted of; nor did he want that relief which could from thence be administered to him.

Besides, had his jewels been missing at the gate of the Celestial City, he had (and that he knew well enough) been excluded from an inheritance there; and that would have been worse to him than the appearance and villainy of ten thousand thieves.

HOPEFUL. Why art thou so tart, my brother? Esau sold his birthright, and that for a mess of pottage, and that birthright was his greatest jewel; and if he, why might not Little-faith do so too?

CHRISTIAN. Esau did sell his birthright indeed, and so do many besides, and by so doing exclude themselves from the chief blessing, as also that caitiff did; but you must put a difference betwixt Esau and Little-faith, and also betwixt their estates. Esau's birthright was typical, but Little-faith's jewels were not so; Esau's belly was his god, but Little-faith's belly was not so; Esau's want lay in his fleshly appetite, Little-faith's did not so. Besides, Esau could see no farther than to the fulfilling of his lusts; Behold I am at the point to die (said he), and what profit shall this birthright do me? But Little-faith, though it was his lot to have but a little faith, was by his little faith kept from such extravagances, and made to see and prize his jewels more than to sell them, as Esau did his birthright. You read not anywhere that Esau had faith, no, not so much as a little; therefore no marvel if, where the flesh only bears sway (as it will in that man where no faith is to resist), if he sells his birthright, and his soul and all, and that to the devil of hell; for it is with such, as it is with the ass, who in her occasions cannot be turned away. When their minds are set upon their lusts, they will have them whatever they cost. But Little-faith was of another temper, his mind was on things divine; his livelihood was upon things that were spiritual, and from above; therefore, to what end should he that is of such a temper sell his jewels (had there been any that would have bought them) to fill his mind with empty things? Will a man give a penny to fill his belly with hay; or can you persuade the turtle-dove to live upon carrion like the crow? Though faithless ones can, for carnal lusts, pawn, or mortgage, or sell what they have, and themselves outright to boot; yet they that have faith, saving faith, though but a little of it, cannot do so. Here, therefore, my brother, is thy mistake.

HOPEFUL. I acknowledge it; but yet your severe reflection had almost made me angry.

CHRISTIAN. Why, I did but compare thee to some of the birds that are of the brisker sort, who will run to and fro in untrodden paths, with the shell upon their heads; but pass by that, and consider the matter under debate, and all shall be well betwixt thee and me.

HOPEFUL. But, Christian, these three fellows, I am persuaded in my heart, are but a company of cowards; would they have run else, think you, as they did, at the noise of one that was coming on the road? Why did not Little-faith pluck up a greater heart? He might, methinks, have stood one brush with them, and have yielded when there had been no remedy.

CHRISTIAN. That they are cowards, many have said, but few have found it so in the time of trial. As for a great heart, Little-faith had none; and I perceive by thee, my brother, hadst thou been the man concerned, thou art but for a brush, and then to yield. And, verily, since this is the height of thy stomach, now they are at a distance from us, should they appear to thee as they did to him, they might put thee to second thoughts.

But, consider again, they are but journeymen thieves, they serve under the king of the bottomless pit, who, if need be, will come in to their aid himself, and his voice is as the roaring lion. I myself have been engaged as this Little-faith was, and I found it a terrible thing. These three villains set upon me, and I beginning, like a Christian, to resist, they gave but a call, and in came their masters. I would, as the saying is, have given my life for a penny; but that, as God would have it, I was clothed with armour of proof. Aye, and yet, though I was so harnessed, I found it hard work to quit myself like a man. No man can tell what in that combat attends us, but he that hath been in the battle himself.

HOPEFUL. Well, but they ran, you see, when they did but suppose that one Great-grace was in the way.

CHRISTIAN. True, they have often fled, both they and their master, when Great-grace hath but appeared; and no marvel; for he is the King's Champion. But, I trow, you will put some difference betwixt Little-faith and the King's Champion. All the King's subjects are not his champions, nor can they, when tried, do such feats of war as he. Is it meet to think that a little child should handle Goliath as David did? Or that there should be the strength of an ox in a wren? Some are strong, some are weak; some have great faith, some have little. This man was one of the weak, and therefore he went to the wall.

HOPEFUL. I would it had been Great-grace for their sakes.

CHRISTIAN. If it had been, he might have had his hands full; for I must tell you, that though Great-grace is excellent good at his weapons, and has, and can, so long as he keeps them at sword's point, do well enough with them; yet, if they get within him, even Faint-heart, Mistrust, or the other, it shall go hard but they will throw up his heels. And when a man is down, you know, what can he do?

Whoso looks well upon Great-grace's face, shall see those scars and cuts there, that shall easily give demonstration of what I say. Yea, once I heard that he should say (and that when he was in the combat), We despaired even of life. How did these sturdy rogues and their fellows make David groan, mourn, and roar? Yea, Heman and Hezekiah, too, though champions in their day, were forced to bestir them, when by these assaulted; and yet, notwithstanding, they had their coats soundly brushed by them. Peter, upon a time, would go try what he could do; but though some do say of him that he is the prince of the apostles, they handled him so, that they made him at last afraid of a sorry girl.

Besides, their king is at their whistle. He is never out of hearing; and if at any time they be put to the worst, he, if possible, comes in to help them; and of him it is said, The sword of him that layeth at him cannot hold; the spear, the dart, nor the habergeon: he esteemeth iron as straw, and brass as rotten wood. The arrow cannot make him flee; sling-stones are turned with him into stubble. Darts are counted as stubble: he laugheth at the shaking of a spear. What can a man do in this case? It is true, if a man could, at every turn, have Job's horse, and had skill and courage to ride him, he might do notable things; 'for his neck is clothed with thunder, he will not be afraid as the grasshopper; the glory of his nostrils is terrible; he paweth in the valley, and rejoiceth in his strength, he goeth on to meet the armed men. He mocketh at fear, and is not affrighted, neither turneth he back from the sword. The quiver rattleth against him, the glittering spear, and the shield. He swalloweth the ground with fierceness and rage, neither believeth he that it is the sound of the trumpet. He saith among the trumpets, Ha, ha! and he smelleth the battle afar off, the thunder of the captains, and the shouting.'

But for such footmen as thou and I are, let us never desire to meet with an enemy, nor vaunt as if we could do better, when we hear of others that they have been foiled, nor be tickled at the thoughts of our own manhood; for such commonly come by the worst when tried. Witness Peter, of whom I made mention before. He would swagger, aye, he would; he would, as his vain mind prompted him to say, do better, and stand more for his Master than all men; but who so foiled, and run down by these villains, as he?

When, therefore, we hear that such robberies are done on the King's highway, two things become us to do: 1. To go out harnessed, and to be sure to take a shield with us; for it was for want of that, that he that laid so lustily at Leviathan could not make him yield; for, indeed, if that be wanting, he fears us not at all. Therefore, he that had skill hath said, Above all, taking the shield of faith, wherewith ye shall be able to quench all the fiery darts of the wicked.

2. It is good, also, that we desire of the King a convoy, yea, that he will go with us himself. This made David rejoice when in the Valley of the Shadow of Death; and Moses was rather for dying where he stood, than to go one step without his God. O my brother, if he will but go along with us, what need we be afraid of ten thousands that shall set themselves against us? But, without him, the proud helpers fall under the slain.

I, for my part, have been in the fray before now; and though, through the goodness of him that is best, I am, as you see, alive; yet I cannot boast of my manhood. Glad shall I be, if I meet with no more such brunts; though, I fear, we are not got beyond all danger. However, since the lion and the bear have not as yet devoured me, I hope God will also deliver us from the next uncircumcised Philistine. Then sang Christian:

> Poor Little-faith! Hast been among the thieves?
> Wast robb'd? Remember this, whoso believes,
> And gets more faith, shall then a victor be
> Over ten thousand, else scarce over three.

So they went on, and Ignorance followed. They went then till they came at a place where they saw a way put itself into their way, and seemed withal to lie as straight as the way which they should go; and here they knew not which of the two to take, for both seemed straight before them; therefore, here they stood still to consider. And as they were thinking about the way, behold a man, black of flesh, but covered with a very light robe, came to them, and asked them why they stood there. They answered, they were going to the Celestial City, but knew not which of these ways to take. Follow me, said the man, it is thither that I am going. So they followed him in the way that but now came into the road, which by degrees turned, and turned them so from the city that they desired to go to, that, in little time, their faces were turned away from it; yet they followed him. But by and by, before they were aware, he led them both within the compass of a net, in which they were both so entangled, that they knew not what to do; and with that the white robe fell off the black man's back. Then they saw where they were. Wherefore, there they lay crying some time, for they could not get themselves out.

CHRISTIAN. Then said Christian to his fellow, Now do I see myself in an error. Did not the Shepherds bid us beware of the flatterers? As is the saying of the wise man, so we have found it this day, A man that flattereth his neighbour, spreadeth a net for his feet.

HOPEFUL. They also gave us a note of directions about the way, for our more sure finding thereof; but therein we have also forgotten to read, and have not kept ourselves from the paths of the destroyer. Here David was wiser than we; for, saith he, Concerning the works of men, by the word of thy lips, I have kept me from the paths of the destroyer. Thus they lay bewailing themselves in the net. At last they espied a Shining One coming towards them, with a whip of small cord in his hand. When he was come to the place where they were, he asked them whence they came, and what they did there. They told him that they were poor pilgrims going to Zion, but were led out of their way by a black man, clothed in white, who bid us, said they, follow him, for he was going thither too. Then said he with the whip, It is Flatterer, a false apostle, that hath transformed himself into an angel of light. So he rent the net, and let the men out. Then said he to them, Follow me, that I may set you in your way again. So he led them back to the way which they had left to follow the Flatterer. Then he asked them, saying, Where did you lie the last night? They said, With the Shepherds, upon the Delectable Mountains. He asked them then, if they had not of those Shepherds a note of direction for the way. They answered, Yes. But did you, said he, when you were at a stand, pluck out and read your note? They answered, No. He asked them, Why? They said, they forgot. He asked, moreover, if the Shepherds did not bid them beware of the Flatterer. They answered, Yes, but we did not imagine, said they, that this fine-spoken man had been he.

Then I saw in my dream, that he commanded them to lie down; which, when they did, he chastised them sore, to teach them the good way wherein they should walk; and as he chastised them, he said, As many as I love, I rebuke and chasten; be zealous, therefore, and repent. This done, he bid them go on their way, and take good heed to the other directions of the Shepherds. So they thanked him for all his kindness, and went softly along the right way, singing:

> Come hither, you that walk along the way;
> See how the pilgrims fare that go astray!
> They catched are in an entangling net,
> 'Cause they good counsel lightly did forget:
> 'Tis true, they rescued were, but yet you see,
> They're scourg'd to boot. Let this your caution be.

Now, after a while, they perceived, afar off, one coming softly and alone, all along the highway to meet them. Then said Christian to his fellow, Yonder is a man with his back toward Zion, and he is coming to meet us.

HOPEFUL. I see him, let us take heed to ourselves now, lest he should prove a flatterer also. So he drew nearer and nearer, and at last came up unto them. His name was Atheist, and he asked them whither they were going.

CHRISTIAN. We are going to the Mount Zion.

Then Atheist fell into a very great laughter.

CHRISTIAN. What is the meaning of your laughter?

ATHEIST. I laugh to see what ignorant persons you are, to take upon you so tedious a journey, and yet are like to have nothing but your travel for your pains.

CHRISTIAN. Why, man, do you think we shall not be received?

ATHEIST. Received! There is no such place as you dream of in all this world.

CHRISTIAN. But there is in the world to come.

ATHEIST. When I was at home in mine own country, I heard as you now affirm, and from that hearing went out to see, and have been seeking this city this twenty years; but find no more of it than I did the first day I set out.

CHRISTIAN. We have both heard and believe that there is such a place to be found.

ATHEIST. Had not I, when at home, believed, I had not come thus far to seek; but finding none (and yet I should, had there been such a place to be found, for I have gone to seek it farther than you), I am going back again, and will seek to refresh myself with the things that I then cast away, for hopes of that which, I now see, is not.

CHRISTIAN. Then said Christian to Hopeful his fellow, Is it true which this man hath said?

HOPEFUL. Take heed, he is one of the flatterers; remember what it hath cost us once already for our hearkening to such kind of fellows. What! no

Mount Zion? Did we not see, from the Delectable Mountains, the gate of the city? Also, are we not now to walk by faith? Let us go on, said Hopeful, lest the man with the whip overtake us again.

You should have taught me that lesson, which I will round you in the ears withal: Cease, my son, to hear the instruction that causeth to err from the words of knowledge. I say, my brother, cease to hear him, and let us believe to the saving of the soul.

CHRISTIAN. My brother, I did not put the question to thee, for that I doubted of the truth of our belief myself, but to prove thee, and to fetch from thee a fruit of the honesty of thy heart. As for this man, I know that he is blinded by the god of this world. Let thee and me go on, knowing that we have belief of the truth, and no lie is of the truth.

HOPEFUL. Now do I rejoice in hope of the glory of God. So they turned away from the man; and he, laughing at them, went his way.

I saw then in my dream, that they went till they came into a certain country, whose air naturally tended to make one drowsy, if he came a stranger into it. And here Hopeful began to be very dull and heavy of sleep; wherefore he said unto Christian, I do now begin to grow so drowsy that I can scarcely hold up mine eyes; let us lie down here, and take one nap.

CHRISTIAN. By no means, said the other; lest, sleeping, we never awake more.

HOPEFUL. Why, my brother? Sleep is sweet to the labouring man; we may be refreshed if we take a nap.

CHRISTIAN. Do you not remember that one of the Shepherds bid us beware of the Inchanted Ground? He meant by that, that we should beware of sleeping; Therefore let us not sleep, as do others, but let us watch and be sober.

HOPEFUL. I acknowledge myself in a fault; and had I been here alone, I had by sleeping run the danger of death. I see it is true that the wise man saith, Two are better than one. Hitherto hath thy company been my mercy, and thou shalt have a good reward for thy labour.

CHRISTIAN. Now then, said Christian, to prevent drowsiness in this place, let us fall into good discourse.

HOPEFUL. With all my heart, said the other.

CHRISTIAN. Where shall we begin?

HOPEFUL. Where God began with us. But do you begin, if you please.

CHRISTIAN. I will sing you first this song:

> When saints do sleepy grow, let them come hither,
> And hear how these two pilgrims talk together;
> Yea, let them learn of them, in any wise,
> Thus to keep ope their drowsy slumb'ring eyes.
> Saints' fellowship, if it be manag'd well,
> Keeps them awake, and that in spite of hell.

CHRISTIAN. Then Christian began, and said, I will ask you a question. How came you to think at first of so doing as you do now?

HOPEFUL. Do you mean, how came I at first to look after the good of my soul?

CHRISTIAN. Yes, that is my meaning.

HOPEFUL. I continued a great while in the delight of those things which were seen and sold at our fair; things which, I believe now, would have, had I continued in them still, drowned me in perdition and destruction.

CHRISTIAN. What things were they?

HOPEFUL. All the treasures and riches of the world. Also I delighted much in rioting, revelling, drinking, swearing, lying, uncleanness, Sabbath-breaking, and what not, that tended to destroy the soul. But I found at last, by hearing and considering of things that are Divine, which indeed I heard of you, as also of beloved Faithful, that was put to death for his faith and good living in Vanity Fair, that the end of these things is death. And that for these things' sake, cometh the wrath of God upon the children of disobedience.

CHRISTIAN. And did you presently fall under the power of this conviction?

HOPEFUL. No, I was not willing presently to know the evil of sin, nor the damnation that follows upon the commission of it; but endeavoured, when my mind at first began to be shaken with the Word, to shut mine eyes against the light thereof.

CHRISTIAN. But what was the cause of your carrying of it thus to the first workings of God's blessed Spirit upon you?

HOPEFUL. The causes were, 1. I was ignorant that this was the work of God upon me. I never thought that by awakenings for sin, God at first begins the conversion of a sinner. 2. Sin was yet very sweet to my flesh, and I was loath to leave it. 3. I could not tell how to part with mine old companions, their presence and actions were so desirable unto me. 4. The hours in which convictions were upon me, were such troublesome and such heart-affrighting hours, that I could not bear, no not so much as the remembrance of them upon my heart.

CHRISTIAN. Then, as it seems, sometimes you got rid of your trouble?

HOPEFUL. Yes, verily, but it would come into my mind again, and then I should be as bad, nay, worse than I was before.

CHRISTIAN. Why, what was it that brought your sins to mind again?

HOPEFUL. Many things; as,

1. If I did but meet a good man in the streets; or,
2. If I have heard any read in the Bible; or,
3. If mine head did begin to ache; or,
4. If I were told that some of my neighbours were sick; or,
5. If I heard the bell toll for some that were dead; or,
6. If I thought of dying myself; or,
7. If I heard that sudden death happened to others;

8. But especially, when I thought of myself, that I must quickly come to judgment.

CHRISTIAN. And could you at any time, with ease, get off the guilt of sin, when, by any of these ways, it came upon you?

HOPEFUL. No, not I, for then they got faster hold of my conscience; and then, if I did but think of going back to sin (though my mind was turned against it), it would be double torment to me.

CHRISTIAN. And how did you do then?

HOPEFUL. I thought I must endeavour to mend my life; for else, thought I, I am sure to be damned.

CHRISTIAN. And did you endeavour to mend?

HOPEFUL. Yes; and fled from not only my sins, but sinful company too; and betook me to religious duties, as prayer, reading, weeping for sin; speaking truth to my neighbours, etc. These things did I, with many others, too much here to relate.

CHRISTIAN. And did you think yourself well then?

HOPEFUL. Yes, for a while; but, at the last, my trouble came tumbling upon me again, and that over the neck of all my reformations.

CHRISTIAN. How came that about, since you were now reformed?

HOPEFUL. There were several things brought it upon me, especially such sayings as these: All our righteousnesses are as filthy rags. By the works of the law shall no flesh be justified. When ye shall have done all those things, say, We are unprofitable; with many more such like. From whence I began to reason with myself thus: If all my righteousnesses are filthy rags; if, by the deeds of the law, no man can be justified; and if, when we have done all, we are yet unprofitable, then it is but a folly to think of heaven by the law. I further thought thus: If a man runs a hundred pounds into the shop-keeper's debt, and after that shall pay for all that he shall fetch; yet, if this old debt stands still in the book uncrossed, for that the shopkeeper may sue him, and cast him into prison till he shall pay the debt.

CHRISTIAN. Well, and how did you apply this to yourself?

HOPEFUL. Why, I thought thus with myself: I have, by my sins, run a great way into God's book, and that my now reforming will not pay off that score; therefore I should think still, under all my present amendments, But how shall I be freed from that damnation that I have brought myself in danger of, by my former transgressions?

CHRISTIAN. A very good application; but, pray, go on.

HOPEFUL. Another thing that hath troubled me, even since my late amendments, is, that if I look narrowly into the best of what I do now, I still see sin, new sin, mixing itself with the best of that I do; so that now I am forced to conclude, that notwithstanding my former fond conceits of myself and duties, I have committed sin enough in one duty to send me to hell, though my former life had been faultless.

CHRISTIAN. And what did you do then?

HOPEFUL. Do! I could not tell what to do, until I brake my mind to Faithful, for he and I were well acquainted. And he told me, that unless I could

70

obtain the righteousness of a man that never had sinned, neither mine own, nor all the righteousness of the world, could save me.

CHRISTIAN. And did you think he spake true?

HOPEFUL. Had he told me so when I was pleased and satisfied with mine own amendment, I had called him fool for his pains; but now, since I see mine own infirmity, and the sin that cleaves to my best performance, I have been forced to be of his opinion.

CHRISTIAN. But did you think, when at first he suggested it to you, that there was such a man to be found, of whom it might justly be said, that he never committed sin?

HOPEFUL. I must confess the words at first sounded strangely but after a little more talk and company with him, I had full conviction about it.

CHRISTIAN. And did you ask him what man this was, and how you must be justified by him?

HOPEFUL. Yes, and he told me it was the Lord Jesus, that dwelleth on the right hand of the Most High. And thus, said he, you must be justified by him even by trusting to what he hath done by himself in the days of his flesh, and suffered when he did hang on the tree. I asked him further, how that man's righteousness could be of that efficacy to justify another before God? And he told me he was the mighty God, and did what he did, and died the death also, not for himself, but for me; to whom his doings, and the worthiness of them, should be imputed, if I believed on him.

CHRISTIAN. And what did you do then?

HOPEFUL. I made my objections against my believing, for that I thought he was not willing to save me.

CHRISTIAN. And what said Faithful to you then?

HOPEFUL. He bid me go to him and see. Then said I it was presumption; but he said, No, for I was invited to come. Then he gave me a book of Jesus, his inditing, to encourage me the more freely to come; and he said, concerning that book, that every jot and tittle thereof stood firmer than heaven and earth. Then I asked him, What I must do when I came; and he told me, I must entreat upon my knees, with all my heart and soul, the Father to reveal him to me. Then I asked him further, how I must make my supplication to him? And he said, Go, and thou shalt find him upon a mercy-seat, where he sits all the year long, to give pardon and forgiveness to them that come. I told him that I knew not what to say when I came. And he bid me say to this effect, God be merciful to me a sinner, and make me to know and believe in Jesus Christ; for I see, that if his righteousness had not been, or I have not faith in that righteousness, I am utterly cast away. Lord, I have heard that thou art a merciful God, and hast ordained that thy Son Jesus Christ should be the Saviour of the world; and moreover, that thou art willing to bestow him upon such a poor sinner as I am (and I am a sinner indeed), Lord, take therefore this opportunity, and magnify thy grace in the salvation of my soul, through thy Son Jesus Christ. Amen.

CHRISTIAN. And did you do as you were bidden?

HOPEFUL. Yes; over, and over, and over.

71

CHRISTIAN. And did the Father reveal his Son to you?

HOPEFUL. Not at the first, nor second, nor third, nor fourth, nor fifth; no, nor at the sixth time neither.

CHRISTIAN. What did you do then?

HOPEFUL. What! why I could not tell what to do.

CHRISTIAN. Had you not thoughts of leaving off praying?

HOPEFUL. Yes, an hundred times twice told.

CHRISTIAN. And what was the reason you did not?

HOPEFUL. I believed that that was true which had been told me, to wit, that without the righteousness of this Christ, all the world could not save me; and therefore, thought I with myself, if I leave off I die, and I can but die at the throne of grace. And withal, this came into my mind, Though it tarry, wait for it; because it will surely come, it will not tarry. So I continued praying until the Father showed me his Son.

CHRISTIAN. And how was he revealed unto you?

HOPEFUL. I did not see him with my bodily eyes, but with the eyes of my understanding; and thus it was: One day I was very sad, I think sadder than at any one time in my life, and this sadness was through a fresh sight of the greatness and vileness of my sins. And as I was then looking for nothing but hell, and the everlasting damnation of my soul, suddenly, as I thought, I saw the Lord Jesus look down from heaven upon me, and saying, Believe an the Lord Jesus Christ, and thou shalt be saved.

But I replied, Lord, I am a great, a very great sinner. And he answered, My grace is sufficient for thee. Then I said, But, Lord, what is believing? And then I saw from that saying, He that cometh to me shall never hunger, and he that believeth on me shall never thirst; that believing and coming was all one; and that he that came, that is, ran out in his heart and affections after salvation by Christ, he indeed believed in Christ. Then the water stood in mine eyes, and I asked further, But, Lord, may such a great sinner as I am, be indeed accepted of thee, and be saved by thee? And I heard him say, And him that cometh to me, I will in no wise cast out. Then I said, But how, Lord, must I consider of thee in my coming to thee, that my faith may be placed aright upon thee? Then he said, Christ Jesus came into the world to save sinners. He is the end of the law for righteousness to every one that believeth. He died for our sins, and rose again for our justification. He loved us, and washed us from our sins in his own blood. He is mediator betwixt God and us. He ever liveth to make intercession for us. From all which I gathered, that I must look for righteousness in his person, and for satisfaction for my sins by his blood; that what he did in obedience to his Father's law, and in submitting to the penalty thereof, was not for himself, but for him that will accept it for his salvation, and be thankful. And now was my heart full of joy, mine eyes full of tears, and mine affections running over with love to the name, people, and ways of Jesus Christ.

CHRISTIAN. This was a revelation of Christ to your soul indeed; but tell me particularly what effect this had upon your spirit.

HOPEFUL. It made me see that all the world, notwithstanding all the righteousness thereof, is in a state of condemnation. It made me see that God the Father, though he be just, can justly justify the coming sinner. It made me greatly ashamed of the vileness of my former life, and confounded me with the sense of mine own ignorance; for there never came thought into my heart before now, that showed me so the beauty of Jesus Christ. It made me love a holy life, and long to do something for the honour and glory of the name of the Lord Jesus; yea, I thought that had I now a thousand gallons of blood in my body, I could spill it all for the sake of the Lord Jesus.

I saw then in my dream that Hopeful looked back and saw Ignorance, whom they had left behind, coming after. Look, said he to Christian, how far yonder youngster loitereth behind.

CHRISTIAN. Aye, aye, I see him; he careth not for our company.

HOPEFUL. But I trow it would not have hurt him, had he kept pace with us hitherto.

CHRISTIAN. That is true; but I warrant you he thinketh otherwise.

HOPEFUL. That I think he doth; but, however, let us tarry for him. So they did.

Then Christian said to him, Come away, man, why do you stay so behind?

IGNORANCE. I take my pleasure in walking alone, even more a great deal than in company, unless I like it the better.

Then said Christian to Hopeful (but softly), Did not I tell you he cared not for our company? But, however, said he, come up, and let us talk away the time in this solitary place. Then, directing his speech to Ignorance, he said, Come, how do you? How stands it between God and your soul now?

IGNORANCE. I hope well; for I am always full of good motions, that come into my mind, to comfort me as I walk.

CHRISTIAN. What good motions? pray tell us.

IGNORANCE. Why, I think of God and heaven.

CHRISTIAN. So do the devils and damned souls.

IGNORANCE. But I think of them, and desire them.

CHRISTIAN. So do many that are never like to come there. The soul of the sluggard desireth, and hath nothing.

IGNORANCE. But I think of them, and leave all for them.

CHRISTIAN. That I doubt; for leaving all is a hard matter; yea, a harder matter than many are aware of. But why, or by what, art thou persuaded that thou hast left all for God and heaven?

IGNORANCE. My heart tells me so.

CHRISTIAN. The wise man says, He that trusts his own heart is a fool.

IGNORANCE. This is spoken of an evil heart, but mine is a good one.

CHRISTIAN. But how dost thou prove that?

IGNORANCE. It comforts me in hopes of heaven.

CHRISTIAN. That may be through its deceitfulness; for a man's heart may minister comfort to him in the hopes of that thing for which he yet has no ground to hope.

IGNORANCE. But my heart and life agree together, and therefore my hope is well grounded.

CHRISTIAN. Who told thee that thy heart and life agree together?

IGNORANCE. My heart tells me so.

CHRISTIAN. Ask my fellow if I be a thief! Thy heart tells thee so! Except the Word of God beareth witness in this matter, other testimony is of no value.

IGNORANCE. But is it not a good heart that hath good thoughts? and is not that a good life that is according to God's commandments?

CHRISTIAN. Yes, that is a good heart that hath good thoughts, and that is a good life that is according to God's commandments; but it is one thing, indeed, to have these, and another thing only to think so.

IGNORANCE. Pray, what count you good thoughts, and a life according to God's commandments?

CHRISTIAN. There are good thoughts of divers kinds; some respecting ourselves, some God, some Christ, and some other things.

IGNORANCE. What be good thoughts respecting ourselves?

CHRISTIAN. Such as agree with the Word of God.

IGNORANCE. When do our thoughts of ourselves agree with the Word of God?

CHRISTIAN. When we pass the same judgment upon ourselves which the Word passes. To explain myself—the Word of God saith of persons in a natural condition, There is none righteous, there is none that doeth good. It saith also, that every imagination of the heart of man is only evil, and that continually. And again, The imagination of man's heart is evil from his youth. Now then, when we think thus of ourselves, having sense thereof, then are our thoughts good ones, because according to the Word of God.

IGNORANCE. I will never believe that my heart is thus bad.

CHRISTIAN. Therefore thou never hadst one good thought concerning thyself in thy life. But let me go on. As the Word passeth a judgment upon our heart, so it passeth a judgment upon our ways; and when our thoughts of our hearts and ways agree with the judgment which the Word giveth of both, then are both good, because agreeing thereto.

IGNORANCE. Make out your meaning.

CHRISTIAN. Why, the Word of God saith that man's ways are crooked ways; not good, but perverse. It saith they are naturally out of the good way, that they have not known it. Now, when a man thus thinketh of his ways; I say, when he doth sensibly, and with heart humiliation, thus think, then hath he good thoughts of his own ways, because his thoughts now agree with the judgment of the Word of God.

IGNORANCE. What are good thoughts concerning God?

CHRISTIAN. Even as I have said concerning ourselves, when our thoughts of God do agree with what the Word saith of him; and that is, when we think of his being and attributes as the Word hath taught, of which I cannot now discourse at large; but to speak of him with reference to us: Then we have right thoughts of God, when we think that he knows us better than we know ourselves, and can see sin in us when and where we can see none in ourselves; when we think he knows our inmost thoughts, and that our heart, with all its depths, is always open unto his eyes; also, when we think that all our righteousness stinks in his nostrils, and that, therefore, he cannot abide to see us stand before him in any confidence, even in all our best performances.

IGNORANCE. Do you think that I am such a fool as to think God can see no farther than I? or, that I would come to God in the best of my performances?

CHRISTIAN. Why, how dost thou think in this matter?

IGNORANCE. Why, to be short, I think I must believe in Christ for justification.

CHRISTIAN. How! think thou must believe in Christ, when thou seest not thy need of him! Thou neither seest thy original nor actual infirmities; but hast such an opinion of thyself, and of what thou dost, as plainly renders thee to be one that did never see a necessity of Christ's personal righteousness to justify thee before God. How, then, dost thou say, I believe in Christ?

IGNORANCE. I believe well enough for all that.

CHRISTIAN. How dost thou believe?

IGNORANCE. I believe that Christ died for sinners; and that I shall be justified before God from the curse, through his gracious acceptance of my obedience to his law. Or thus, Christ makes my duties, that are religious, acceptable to his father, by virtue of his merits; and so shall I be justified.

CHRISTIAN. Let me give an answer to this confession of thy faith.

1. Thou believest with a fantastical faith; for this faith is nowhere described in the Word.

2. Thou believest with a false faith; because it taketh justification from the personal righteousness of Christ, and applies it to thy own.

3. This faith maketh not Christ a justifier of thy person, but of thy actions; and of thy person for thy actions' sake, which is false.

4. Therefore, this faith is deceitful, even such as will leave thee under wrath, in the day of God Almighty; for true justifying faith puts the soul, as sensible of its lost condition by the law, upon flying for refuge unto Christ's righteousness, which righteousness of his is not an act of grace, by which he maketh, for justification, thy obedience accepted with God; but his personal obedience to the law, in doing and suffering for us what that required at our hands; his righteousness, I say, true faith accepteth; under the skirt of which, the soul being shrouded, and by it presented as spotless before God, it is accepted, and acquit from condemnation.

IGNORANCE. What! would you have us trust to what Christ, in his own person, has done without us? This conceit would loosen the reins of our lust, and tolerate us to live as we list; for what matter how we live, if we may be justified by Christ's personal righteousness from all, when we believe it?

CHRISTIAN. Ignorance is thy name, and as thy name is, so art thou; even this thy answer demonstrateth what I say. Ignorant thou art of what justifying righteousness is, and as ignorant how to secure thy soul, through the faith of it, from the heavy wrath of God. Yea, thou also art ignorant of the true effects of saving faith in this righteousness of Christ, which is, to bow and win over the heart to God in Christ, to love his name, his Word, ways, and people, and not as thou ignorantly imaginest.

HOPEFUL. Ask him if ever he had Christ revealed to him from heaven.

IGNORANCE. What! you are a man for revelations! I believe that what both you, and all the rest of you, say about that matter, is but the fruit of distracted brains.

HOPEFUL. Why, man! Christ is so hid in God from the natural apprehensions of the flesh, that he cannot by any man be savingly known, unless God the Father reveals him to them.

IGNORANCE. That is your faith, but not mine; yet mine, I doubt not, is as good as yours, though I have not in my head so many whimsies as you.

CHRISTIAN. Give me leave to put in a word. You ought not so slightly to speak of this matter; for this I will boldly affirm, even as my good companion hath done, that no man can know Jesus Christ, but by the revelation of the Father; yea, and faith too, by which the soul layeth hold upon Christ, if it be right, must be wrought by the exceeding greatness of his mighty power; the working of which faith, I perceive, poor Ignorance, thou art ignorant of. Be awakened then, see thine own wretchedness, and fly to the Lord Jesus; and by his righteousness, which is the righteousness of God, for he himself is God, thou shalt be delivered from condemnation.

IGNORANCE. You go so fast, I cannot keep pace with you. Do you go on before; I must stay a while behind.

Then they said:

> Well, Ignorance, wilt thou yet foolish be,
> To slight good counsel, ten times given thee?
> And if thou yet refuse it, thou shalt know,
> Ere long, the evil of thy doing so.
> Remember, man, in time, stoop, do not fear;
> Good counsel taken well, saves: therefore hear.
> But if thou yet shalt slight it, thou wilt be
> The loser (Ignorance) I'll warrant thee.

Then Christian addressed thus himself to his fellow:

CHRISTIAN. Well, come, my good Hopeful, I perceive that thou and I must walk by ourselves again.

So I saw in my dream that they went on apace before, and Ignorance he came hobbling after. Then said Christian to his companion, It pities me much for this poor man, it will certainly go ill with him at last.

HOPEFUL. Alas! there are abundance in our town in his condition, whole families, yes, whole streets, and that of pilgrims too; and if there be so many in our parts, how many, think you, must there be in the place where he was born?

76

CHRISTIAN. Indeed the Word saith, He hath blinded their eyes, lest they should see, etc. But now we are by ourselves, what do you think of such men? Have they at no time, think you, convictions of sin, and so consequently fears that their state is dangerous?

HOPEFUL. Nay, do you answer that question yourself, for you are the elder man.

CHRISTIAN. Then I say, sometimes (as I think) they may; but they being naturally ignorant, understand not that such convictions tend to their good; and therefore they do desperately seek to stifle them, and presumptuously continue to flatter themselves in the way of their own hearts.

HOPEFUL. I do believe, as you say, that fear tends much to men's good, and to make them right, at their beginning to go on pilgrimage.

CHRISTIAN. Without all doubt it doth, if it be right; for so says the Word, The fear of the Lord is the beginning of wisdom.

HOPEFUL. How will you describe right fear?

CHRISTIAN. True or right fear is discovered by three things:

1. By its rise; it is caused by saving convictions for sin.

2. It driveth the soul to lay fast hold of Christ for salvation.

3. It begetteth and continueth in the soul a great reverence of God, his Word, and ways, keeping it tender, and making it afraid to turn from them, to the right hand or to the left, to anything that may dishonour God, break its peace, grieve the Spirit, or cause the enemy to speak reproachfully.

HOPEFUL. Well said; I believe you have said the truth. Are we now almost got past the Inchanted Ground?

CHRISTIAN. Why, art thou weary of this discourse?

HOPEFUL. No, verily, but that I would know where we are.

CHRISTIAN. We have not now above two miles further to go thereon. But let us return to our matter. Now the ignorant know not that such convictions as tend to put them in fear are for their good, and therefore they seek to stifle them.

HOPEFUL. How do they seek to stifle them?

CHRISTIAN. 1. They think that those fears are wrought by the devil (though indeed they are wrought of God); and, thinking so, they resist them as things that directly tend to their overthrow. 2. They also think that these fears tend to the spoiling of their faith, when, alas for them, poor men that they are, they have none at all! and therefore they harden their hearts against them. 3. They presume they ought not to fear; and therefore, in despite of them, wax presumptuously confident. 4. They see that those fears tend to take away from them their pitiful old self-holiness, and therefore they resist them with all their might.

HOPEFUL. I know something of this myself; for, before I knew myself, it was so with me.

CHRISTIAN. Well, we will leave, at this time, our neighbour Ignorance by himself, and fall upon another profitable question.

HOPEFUL. With all my heart, but you shall still begin.

CHRISTIAN. Well then, did you not know, about ten years ago, one Temporary in your parts, who was a forward man in religion then?

HOPEFUL. Know him! yes, he dwelt in Graceless, a town about two miles off of Honesty, and he dwelt next door to one Turnback.

CHRISTIAN. Right, he dwelt under the same roof with him. Well, that man was much awakened once; I believe that then he had some sight of his sins, and of the wages that were due thereto.

HOPEFUL. I am of your mind, for, my house not being above three miles from him, he would ofttimes come to me, and that with many tears. Truly I pitied the man, and was not altogether without hope of him; but one may see, it is not every one that cries, Lord, Lord.

CHRISTIAN. He told me once that he was resolved to go on pilgrimage, as we do now; but all of a sudden he grew acquainted with one Save-self, and then he became a stranger to me.

HOPEFUL. Now, since we are talking about him, let us a little enquire into the reason of the sudden backsliding of him and such others.

CHRISTIAN. It may be very profitable, but do you begin.

HOPEFUL. Well then, there are in my judgment four reasons for it:

1. Though the consciences of such men are awakened, yet their minds are not changed; therefore, when the power of guilt weareth away, that which provoked them to be religious ceaseth, wherefore they naturally turn to their own course again, even as we see the dog that is sick of what he has eaten, so long as his sickness prevails, he vomits and casts up all; not that he doth this of a free mind (if we may say a dog has a mind), but because it troubleth his stomach; but now, when his sickness is over, and so his stomach eased, his desire being not at all alienate from his vomit, he turns him about and licks up all, and so it is true which is written, The dog is turned to his own vomit again. Thus I say, being hot for heaven, by virtue only of the sense and fear of the torments of hell, as their sense of hell, and the fears of damnation, chills and cools, so their desires for heaven and salvation cool also. So then it comes to pass, that when their guilt and fear is gone, their desires for heaven and happiness die, and they return to their course again.

2. Another reason is, they have slavish fears that do overmaster them; I speak now of the fears that they have of men, for the fear of man bringeth a snare. So then, though they seem to be hot for heaven, so long as the flames of hell are about their ears, yet, when that terror is a little over, they betake themselves to second thoughts; namely, that it is good to be wise, and not to run (for they know not what) the hazard of losing all, or, at least, of bringing themselves into unavoidable and unnecessary troubles, and so they fall in with the world again.

3. The shame that attends religion lies also as a block in their way; they are proud and haughty, and religion in their eye is low and contemptible; therefore, when they have lost their sense of hell and wrath to come, they return again to their former course.

4. Guilt, and to meditate terror, are grievous to them. They like not to

see their misery before they come into it; though perhaps the sight of it first, if they loved that sight, might make them fly whither the righteous fly and are safe. But because they do, as I hinted before, even shun the thoughts of guilt and terror, therefore, when once they are rid of their awakenings about the terrors and wrath of God, they harden their hearts gladly, and choose such ways as will harden them more and more.

CHRISTIAN. You are pretty near the business, for the bottom of all is, for want of a change in their mind and will. And therefore they are but like the felon that standeth before the judge; he quakes and trembles, and seems to repent most heartily, but the bottom of all is the fear of the halter; not that he hath any detestation of the offence, as is evident, because, let but this man have his liberty, and he will be a thief, and so a rogue still, whereas, if his mind was changed, he would be otherwise.

HOPEFUL. Now, I have showed you the reasons of their going back, do you show me the manner thereof.

CHRISTIAN. So I will, willingly.

1. They draw off their thoughts, all that they may, from the remembrance of God, death, and judgment to come.

2. Then they cast off by degrees private duties, as closet prayer, curbing their lusts, watching, sorrow for sin, and the like.

3. Then they shun the company of lively and warm Christians.

4. After that, they grow cold to public duty, as hearing, reading, godly conference, and the like.

5. Then they begin to pick holes, as we say, in the coats of some of the godly; and that devilishly, that they may have a seeming colour to throw religion (for the sake of some infirmity they have espied in them) behind their backs.

6. Then they begin to adhere to, and associate themselves with, carnal, loose, and wanton men.

7. Then they give way to carnal and wanton discourses in secret; and glad are they if they can see such things in any that are counted honest, that they may the more boldly do it through their example.

8. After this, they begin to play with little sins openly.

9. And then, being hardened, they show themselves as they are. Thus, being launched again into the gulf of misery, unless a miracle of grave prevent it, they everlastingly perish in their own deceivings.

Now I saw in my dream, that by this time the Pilgrims were got over the Inchanted Ground, and entering into the country of Beulah, whose air was very sweet and pleasant, the way lying directly through it, they solaced themselves there for a season. Yea, here they heard continually the singing of birds, and saw every day the flowers appear in the earth, and heard the voice of the turtle in the land. In this country the sun shineth night and day; wherefore this was beyond the Valley of the Shadow of Death, and also out of the reach of Giant Despair, neither could they from this place so much as see Doubting Castle. Here they were within sight of the city they were going to, also here met them some of the inhabitants thereof;

for in this land the Shining Ones commonly walked, because it was upon the borders of heaven. In this land also the contract between the bride and the bridegroom was renewed; yea, here, as the bridegroom rejoiceth over the bride, so did their God rejoice over them. Here they had no want of corn and wine; for in this place they met with abundance of what they had sought for in all their pilgrimage. Here they heard voices from out of the city, loud voices, saying, Say ye to the daughter of Zion, Behold, thy salvation cometh! Behold, his reward is with him! Here all the inhabitants of the country called them, The holy people, The redeemed of the Lord, Sought out, etc.

Now, as they walked in this land, they had more rejoicing than in parts more remote from the kingdom to which they were bound; and drawing near to the city, they had yet a more perfect view thereof. It was builded of pearls and precious stones, also the street thereof was paved with gold; so that by reason of the natural glory of the city, and the reflection of the sunbeams upon it, Christian with desire fell sick, Hopeful also had a fit or two of the same disease. Wherefore, here they lay by it a while, crying out, because of their pangs, If ye find my Beloved, tell him that I am sick of love.

But being a little strengthened, and better able to bear their sickness, they walked on their way, and came yet nearer and nearer, where were orchards, vineyards, and gardens, and their gates opened into the highway. Now, as they came up to these places, behold, the gardener stood in the way, to whom the Pilgrims said, Whose goodly vineyards and gardens are these? He answered, They are the King's, and are planted here for his own delight, and also for the solace of pilgrims. So the gardener had them into the vineyards, and bid them refresh themselves with the dainties. He also showed them there the King's walks, and the arbours, where he delighted to be; and here they tarried and slept.

Now I beheld in my dream, that they talked more in their sleep at this time than ever they did in all their journey; and being in a muse thereabout, the gardener said even to me, Wherefore musest thou at the matter? It is the nature of the fruit of the grapes of these vineyards to go down so sweetly, as to cause the lips of them that are asleep to speak.

So I saw that when they awoke, they addressed themselves to go up to the city. But, as I said, the reflection of the sun upon the city (for the city was pure gold) was so extremely glorious, that they could not, as yet, with open face behold it, but through an instrument made for that purpose. So I saw, that as they went on, there met them two men, in raiment that shone like gold; also their faces shone as the light.

These men asked the Pilgrims whence they came; and they told them. They also asked them where they had lodged, what difficulties and dangers, what comforts and pleasures they had met in the way; and they told them. Then said the men that met them, You have but two difficulties more to meet with, and then you are in the city.

Christian then, and his companion, asked the men to go along with them; so they told them they would. But, said they, you must obtain it by your

80

own faith. So I saw in my dream that they went on together, until they came in sight of the gate.

Now, I further saw, that betwixt them and the gate was a river, but there was no bridge to go over; the river was very deep. At the sight, therefore, of this river, the Pilgrims were much stunned: but the men that went with them said, You must go through, or you cannot come at the gate.

The Pilgrims then began to enquire if there was no other way to the gate; to which they answered, Yes; but there hath not any, save two, to wit, Enoch and Elijah, been permitted to tread that path, since the foundation of the world, nor shall, until the last trumpet shall sound. The Pilgrims then, especially Christian, began to despond in their minds, and looked this way and that, but no way could be found by them, by which they might escape the river. Then they asked the men if the waters were all of a depth. They said, No; yet they could not help them in that case; for, said they, you shall find it deeper or shallower as you believe in the King of the place.

Then they addressed themselves to the water; and entering, Christian began to sink, and crying out to his good friend Hopeful, he said, I sink in deep waters; the billows go over my head, all his waves go over me! Selah.

Then said the other, Be of good cheer, my brother, I feel the bottom, and it is good. Then said Christian, Ah! my friend, the sorrows of death have compassed me about; I shall not see the land that flows with milk and honey; and with that a great darkness and horror fell upon Christian, so that he could not see before him. Also here he in great measure lost his senses, so that he could neither remember, nor orderly talk of any of those sweet refreshments that he had met with in the way of his pilgrimage. But all the words that he spake still tended to discover that he had horror of mind, and heart fears that he should die in that river, and never obtain entrance in at the gate. Here also, as they that stood by perceived, he was much in the troublesome thoughts of the sins that he had committed, both since and before he began to be a pilgrim. It was also observed that he was troubled with apparitions of hobgoblins and evil spirits; for ever and anon he would intimate so much by words. Hopeful, therefore, here had much ado to keep his brother's head above water; yea, sometimes he would be quite gone down, and then, ere a while, he would rise up again half dead. Hopeful also would endeavour to comfort him, saying, Brother, I see the gate, and men standing by to receive us; but Christian would answer, It is you, it is you they wait for; you have been Hopeful ever since I knew you. And so have you, said he to Christian. Ah, brother! said he, surely if I was right he would now arise to help me; but for my sins he hath brought me into the snare, and hath left me. Then said Hopeful, My brother, you have quite forgot the text, where it is said of the wicked, There are no bands in their death; but their strength is firm. They are not in trouble as other men, neither are they plagued like other men. These troubles and distresses that you go through in these waters are no sign that God hath forsaken you; but are sent to try you, whether you will call to mind that which heretofore you have received of his goodness, and live upon him in your distresses.

Then I saw in my dream, that Christian was in a muse a while. To whom also Hopeful added this word, Be of good cheer, Jesus Christ maketh thee whole; and with that Christian brake out with a loud voice, Oh! I see him again, and he tells me, When thou passest through the waters, I will be with thee; and through the rivers, they shall not overflow thee. Then they both took courage, and the enemy was after that as still as a stone, until they were gone over. Christian therefore presently found ground to stand upon, and so it followed that the rest of the river was but shallow. Thus they got over. Now, upon the bank of the river, on the other side, they saw the two Shining Men again, who there waited for them; wherefore, being come out of the river, they saluted them, saying, We are ministering spirits, sent forth to minister for those that shall be heirs of salvation. Thus they went along towards the gate. Now you must note that the city stood upon a mighty hill, but the Pilgrims went up that hill with ease, because they had these two men to lead them up by the arms; also, they had left their mortal garments behind them in the river, for though they went in with them, they came out without them. They, therefore, went up here with much agility and speed, though the foundation upon which the city was framed was higher than the clouds. They, therefore, went up through the regions of the air, sweetly talking as they went, comforted, because they safely got over the river, and had such glorious companions to attend them.

The talk they had with the Shining Ones was about the glory of the place; who told them that the beauty and glory of it was inexpressible. There, said they, is the Mount Zion, the heavenly Jerusalem, the innumerable company of angels, and the spirits of just men made perfect. You are going now, said they, to the paradise of God, wherein you shall see the tree of life, and eat of the never-fading fruits thereof; and when you come there, you shall have white robes given you, and your walk and talk shall be every day with the King, even all the days of eternity. There you shall not see again such things as you saw when you were in the lower region upon the earth, to wit, sorrow, sickness, affliction, and death, for the former things are passed away. You are now going to Abraham, to Isaac, and Jacob, and to the prophets—men that God hath taken away from the evil to come, and that are now resting upon their beds, each one walking in his righteousness. The men then asked, What must we do in the holy place? To whom it was answered, You must there receive the comforts of all your toil, and have joy for all your sorrow; you must reap what you have sown, even the fruit of all your prayers, and tears, and sufferings for the King by the way. In that place you must wear crowns of gold, and enjoy the perpetual sight and vision of the Holy One, for there you shall see him as he is. There also you shall serve him continually with praise, with shouting, and thanksgiving, whom you desired to serve in the world, though with much difficulty, because of the infirmity of your flesh. There your eyes shall be delighted with seeing, and your ears with hearing the pleasant voice of the Mighty One. There you shall enjoy your friends again, that are gone thither before you; and there you shall with joy receive, even

82

every one that follows into the holy place after you. There also shall you be clothed with glory and majesty, and put into an equipage fit to ride out with the King of glory. When he shall come with sound of trumpet in the clouds, as upon the wings of the wind, you shall come with him; and when he shall sit upon the throne of judgment, you shall sit by him; yea, and when he shall pass sentence upon all the workers of iniquity, let them be angels or men, you also shall have a voice in that judgment, because they were his and your enemies. Also when he shall again return to the city, you shall go too, with sound of trumpet, and be ever with him.

Now, while they were thus drawing towards the gate, behold a company of the heavenly host came out to meet them; to whom it was said, by the other two Shining Ones, These are the men that have loved our Lord when they were in the world, and that have left all for his holy name; and he hath sent us to fetch them, and we have brought them thus far on their desired journey, that they may go in and look their Redeemer in the face with joy. Then the heavenly host gave a great shout, saying, Blessed are they which are called unto the marriage supper of the Lamb. There came out also at this time to meet them, several of the King's trumpeters, clothed in white and shining raiment, who, with melodious noises, and loud, made even the heavens to echo with their sound. These trumpeters saluted Christian and his fellow with ten thousand welcomes from the world; and this they did with shouting, and sound of trumpet.

This done, they compassed them round on every side; some went before, some behind, and some on the right hand, some on the left (as it were to guard them through the upper regions), continually sounding as they went, with melodious noise, in notes on high; so that the very sight was to them that could behold it, as if heaven itself was come down to meet them. Thus, therefore, they walked on together; and as they walked, ever and anon these trumpeters, even with joyful sound, would, by mixing their music with looks and gestures, still signify to Christian and his brother, how welcome they were into their company, and with what gladness they came to meet them; and now were these two men, as it were, in heaven, before they came at it, being swallowed up with the sight of angels, and with hearing of their melodious notes. Here also they had the city itself in view, and they thought they heard all the bells therein to ring, to welcome them thereto. But above all, the warm and joyful thoughts that they had about their own dwelling there, with such company, and that for ever and ever. O by what tongue or pen can their glorious joy be expressed! And thus they came up to the gate.

Now, when they were come up to the gate, there was written over it in letters of gold, Blessed are they that do his commandments, that they may have right to the tree of life, and may enter in through the gates into the city.

Then I saw in my dream, that the Shining Men bid them call at the gate; the which, when they did, some looked from above over the gate, to wit, Enoch, Moses, and Elijah, etc., to whom it was said, These pilgrims are come from the City of Destruction, for the love that they bear to the King of this place; and then the pilgrims gave in unto them each man his certificate, which they had received in the beginning; those, therefore, were carried in to the King, who, when he had read them, said, Where are the men? To whom it was answered, They are standing without the gate. The King then commanded to open the gate, That the righteous nation, said he, which keepeth the truth, may enter in.

Now I saw in my dream that these two men went in at the gate; and lo, as they entered, they were transfigured, and they had raiment put on that shone like gold. There were also men that met them with harps and crowns, and gave them to them—the harps to praise withal, and the crowns in token of honour. Then I heard in my dream that all the bells in the city rang again for joy, and that it was said unto them, ENTER YE INTO THE JOY OF YOUR LORD. I also heard the men themselves, that they sang with a loud voice, saying, BLESSING, AND HONOUR, AND GLORY, AND POWER, BE UNTO HIM THAT SITTETH UPON THE THRONE, AND UNTO THE LAMB, FOR EVER AND EVER.

Now just as the gates were opened to let in the men, I looked in after them, and, behold, the City shone like the sun; the streets also were paved with gold, and in them walked many men, with crowns on their heads, palms in their hands, and golden harps to sing praises withal.

There were also of them that had wings, and they answered one another without intermission, saying, Holy, holy, holy, is the Lord. And after that, they shut up the gates; which, when I had seen, I wished myself among them.

Now while I was gazing upon all these things, I turned my head to look back, and saw Ignorance come up to the river side; but he soon got over, and that without half that difficulty which the other two men met with. For it happened that there was then in that place, one Vain-hope, a ferryman, that with his boat helped him over; so he, as the other I saw, did ascend the hill, to come up to the gate, only he came alone; neither did any man meet him with the least encouragement. When he was come up to the gate, he looked up to the writing that was above, and then began to knock, supposing that entrance should have been quickly administered to him; but he was asked by the men that looked over the top of the gate, Whence came you? and what would you have? He answered, I have eat and drank in the presence of the King, and he has taught in our streets. Then they asked him for his certificate, that they might go in and show it to the King; so he fumbled in his bosom for one, and found none. Then said they, Have you none? But the man answered never a word. So they told the King, but he would not come down to see him, but commanded the two Shining Ones that conducted Christian and Hopeful to the City, to go out and take Ignorance, and bind him hand and foot, and have him away. Then they took him up, and carried him through the air, to the door that I saw in the side of the hill, and put him in there. Then I saw that there was a way to hell, even from the gates of heaven, as well as from the City of Destruction! So I awoke, and behold it was a dream.

84

THE SECOND PART

---

*The manner of the setting out
of Christian's Wife and Children
their dangerous journey
and their safe arrival at the
desired countrey*

COURTEOUS COMPANIONS, some time since, to tell you my dream that I had of Christian the Pilgrim, and of his dangerous journey towards the Celestial Country, was pleasant to me, and profitable to you. I told you then, also, what I saw concerning his wife and children, and how unwilling they were to go with him on pilgrimage, insomuch that he was forced to go on his progress without them; for he durst not run the danger of that destruction which he feared would come by staying with them in the City of Destruction. Wherefore, as I then showed you, he left them and departed.

Now it hath so happened, through the multiplicity of business, that I have been much hindered and kept back from my wonted travels into those parts whence he went, and so could not, till now, obtain an opportunity to make further enquiry after whom he left behind, that I might give you an account of them. But having had some concerns that way of late, I went down again thitherward. Now, having taken up my lodgings in a wood, about a mile off the place, as I slept, I dreamed again.

And as I was in my dream, behold, an aged gentleman came by where I lay; and because he was to go some part of the way that I was travelling, methought I got up and went with him. So as we walked, and as travellers usually do, I was as if we fell into discourse, and our talk happened to be about Christian and his travels; for thus I began with the old man:

Sir, said I, what town is that there below, that lieth on the left hand of our way?

Then said Mr. Sagacity (for that was his name), It is the City of Destruction, a populous place, but possessed with a very ill-conditioned and idle sort of people.

I thought that was that city, quoth I; I went once myself through that town, and, therefore, know that this report you give of it is true.

SAGACITY. Too true; I wish I could speak truth in speaking better of them that dwell therein.

Well, Sir, quoth I, then I perceive you to be a well-meaning man; and so one that takes pleasure to hear and tell of that which is good. Pray, did you never hear what happened to a man some time ago in this town, whose name was Christian, that went on pilgrimage up towards the higher regions?

SAGACITY. Hear of him! Aye, and I also heard of the molestations, troubles, wars, captivities, cries, groans, frights, and fears that he met with and had in his journey; besides, I must tell you, all our country rings of him. There are but few houses that have heard of him and his doings but have sought after and got the records of his pilgrimage.

I dare say, quoth I, I am glad on it; I am glad for the poor man's sake, for that he now has rest from his labour; and for that he now reapeth the benefit of his tears with joy; and for that he has got beyond the gunshot of his enemies, and is out of the reach of them that hate him. I also am glad, for that a rumour of these things is noised abroad in this country; who can tell but that it may work some good effect on some that are left behind? But, pray Sir, while it is fresh in my mind, do you hear anything of his wife and children? Poor hearts! I wonder in my mind what they do.

SAGACITY. Who! Christiana and her sons? They are like to do as well as did Christian himself; for though they all played the fool at the first, and would by no means be persuaded by either the tears or entreaties of Christian, yet second thoughts have wrought wonderfully with them; so they have packed up, and are also gone after him.

Better and better, quoth I. But what! wife and children, and all?

SAGACITY. It is true; I can give you an account of the matter, for I was upon the spot at the instant, and was thoroughly acquainted with the whole affair.

This Christiana (for that was her name from the day that she, with her children, betook themselves to a pilgrim's life), after her husband was gone over the river, and she could hear of him no more, her thoughts began to work in her mind. First, for that she had lost her husband, and for that the loving bond of that relation was utterly broken betwixt them. For you know, said he to me, nature can do no less but entertain the living with many a heavy cogitation in the remembrance of the loss of loving relations. This, therefore, of her husband did cost her many a tear. But this was not all; for Christiana did also begin to consider with herself, whether her unbecoming behaviour towards her husband was not one cause that she saw him no more; and that in such sort he was taken away from her.

Then said she to her children, Sons, we are all undone. I have sinned away your father, and he is gone; he would have had us with him, but I would not go myself. I also have hindered you of life. With that the boys fell all into tears, and cried out to go after their father. O! said Christiana, that it had been but our lot to go with him, then had it fared well with us, beyond what it is like to do now; for though I formerly foolishly imagined, concerning the troubles of your father, that they proceeded of a foolish fancy that he had, or for that he was overrun with melancholy humours; yet now it will not out of my mind but that they sprang from another cause,

86

to wit, for that the Light of light, was given him; by the help of which, as I perceive, he has escaped the snares of death. Then they all wept again, and cried out, O woe worth the day!

The next night Christiana had a dream; and, behold, she saw as if a broad parchment was opened before her, in which were recorded the sum of her ways; and the times, as she thought, looked very black upon her. Then she cried out aloud in her sleep, Lord, have mercy upon me a sinner; and the little children heard her.

Next morning, when she was up, had prayed to God, and talked with her children a while, one knocked hard at the door, to whom she spake out, saying, If thou comest in God's name, come in. So he said, Amen, and opened the door, and saluted her with Peace be to this house. The which, when he had done, he said, Christiana, knowest thou wherefore I am come? Then she blushed and trembled, also her heart began to wax warm with desires to know whence he came, and what was his errand to her. So he said unto her, My name is Secret; I dwell with those that are high. It is talked of, where I dwell, as if thou hadst a desire to go thither; also, there is a report, that thou art aware of the evil thou hast formerly done to thy husband, in hardening of thy heart against his way, and in keeping of these thy babes in their ignorance. Christiana, the Merciful One has sent me to tell thee, that he is a God ready to forgive, and that he taketh delight to multiply to pardon offences. He also would have thee know, that he inviteth thee to come into his presence, to his table, and that he will feed thee with the fat of his house, and with the heritage of Jacob thy father.

Christiana at this was greatly abashed in herself, and bowing her head to the ground, this Visitor proceeded, and said, Christiana, here is also a letter for thee, which I have brought from thy husband's King. So she took it and opened it, but it smelt after the manner of the best perfume; also it was written in letters of gold. The contents of the letter was, That the King would have her do as did Christian her husband; for that was the way to come to his city, and to dwell in his presence with joy for ever. At this the good woman was quite overcome; so she cried out to her visitor, Sir, will you carry me and my children with you, that we also may go and worship this King?

Then said the visitor, Christiana, the bitter is before the sweet. Thou must through troubles, as did he that went before thee, enter this Celestial city. Wherefore I advise thee to do as did Christian thy husband. Go to the wicket-gate yonder, over the plain, for that stands in the head of the way up which thou must go, and I wish thee all good speed. Also I advise that thou put this letter in thy bosom; that thou read therein to thyself, and to thy children, until you have got it by rote of heart, for it is one of the songs that thou must sing while thou art in this house of thy pilgrimage; also this thou must deliver in at the farther gate.

Now I saw in my dream, that this old gentleman, as he told me this story, did himself seem to be greatly affected therewith. He, moreover, proceeded and said, So Christiana called her sons together, and began thus to address herself unto them: My sons, I have, as you may perceive, been of late under much exercise in my soul, about the death of your father; not for that I doubt at all of his happiness, for I am satisfied now that he is well. I have been also much affected with the thoughts of mine own state and yours, which I verily believe is by nature miserable. My carriages, also, to your father in his distress, is a great load to my conscience; for I hardened both my own heart and yours against him, and refused to go with him on pilgrimage.

The thoughts of these things would now kill me outright, but that for a dream which I had last night, and but for the encouragement that this stranger has given me this morning. Come, my children, let us pack up and begone to the gate that leads to the Celestial Country, that we may see your father, and be with him and his companions in peace.

But while they were thus about to be gone, two of the women, that were Christiana's neighbours, came up to her house, and knocked at her door. To whom she said as before, If you come in God's name, come in. At this the women were stunned; for this kind of language they used not to hear, or to perceive to drop from the lips of Christiana. Yet they came in; but, behold, they found the good woman a-preparing to be gone from her house.

So they began and said, Neighbour, pray what is your meaning by this?

Christiana answered and said to the eldest of them, whose name was Mrs. Timorous, I am preparing for a journey. (This Timorous was daughter to him that met Christian upon the Hill Difficulty, and would have had him go back for fear of the lions.)

TIMOROUS. For what journey, I pray you?

CHRISTIANA. Even to go after my good husband. And with that she fell a-weeping.

TIMOROUS. I hope not so, good neighbour; pray, for your poor children's sakes, do not so unwomanly cast away yourself.

CHRISTIANA. Nay, my children shall go with me, not one of them is willing to stay behind.

TIMOROUS. O the madness that has possessed thee and thy husband, to run yourselves upon such difficulties! You have heard, I am sure, what your husband did meet with, even, in a manner, at the first step that he took on his way, as our neighbour Obstinate can yet testify, for he went along with him; yea, and Pliable too, until they, like wise men, were afraid to go any farther. We also heard, over and above, how he met with the lions, Apollyon, the Shadow of Death, and many other things. Nor is the danger that he met with at Vanity Fair to be forgotten by thee; for if he, though a man, was so hard put to it, what canst thou, being but a poor woman, do? Consider also, that these four sweet babes are thy children, thy flesh and thy bones. Wherefore, though thou shouldest be so rash as to cast away thyself; yet, for the sake of the fruit of thy body, keep thou at home.

Then Timorous also reviled her, and said to her fellow, Come, neighbour Mercy, let us leave her in her own hands, since she scorns our counsel and company. But Mercy was at a stand, and could not so readily comply with her neighbour, and that for a twofold reason. First, her bowels yearned over Christiana. So she said within herself, If my neighbour will needs be gone, I will go a little way with her and help her. Secondly, her bowels yearned over her own soul, for what Christiana had said had taken some hold upon her mind. Wherefore she said within herself again, I will yet have more talk with this Christiana, and if I find truth and life in what she shall say, myself with my heart shall also go with her. Wherefore Mercy began thus to reply to her neighbour Timorous.

MERCY. Neighbour, I did, indeed, come with you to see Christiana this morning; and since she is, as you see, a-taking of her last farewell of her country, I think to walk, this sunshine morning, a little way with her, to help her on the way. But she told her not of the second reason, but kept that to herself.

TIMOROUS. Well, I see you have a mind to go a-fooling too, but take heed in time, and be wise. While we are out of danger, we are out; but when we are in, we are in. So Mrs. Timorous returned to her house, and Christiana betook herself to her journey. But when Timorous was got home to her house, she sends for some of her neighbours, to wit, Mrs. Bat's-eyes, Mrs. Inconsiderate, Mrs. Light-mind, and Mrs. Know-nothing. So when they were come to her house, she falls to telling of the story of Christiana and of her intended journey.

Then said Mrs. Know-nothing, And what! do you think she will go?

TIMOROUS. Aye, go she will, whatever come on't; and methinks I know it by this; for that which was my great argument to persuade her to stay at home (to wit, the troubles she was like to meet with in the way) is one great argument with her to put her forward on her journey. For she told me in so many words, The bitter goes before the sweet. Yea, and forasmuch as it so doth, it makes the sweet the sweeter.

MRS. BAT'S-EYES. O, this blind and foolish woman! said she; will she not take warning by her husband's afflictions? For my part, I see, if he was here again, he would rest him content in a whole skin, and never run so many hazards for nothing.

MRS. INCONSIDERATE also replied, saying, Away with such fantastical fools from the town! A good riddance, for my part, I say, of her. Should she stay where she dwells, and retain this her mind, who could live quietly by her? for she will either be dumpish or unneighbourly, or talk of such matters as no wise body can abide; wherefore, for my part, I shall never be sorry for her departure. Let her go, and let better come in her room. It was never a good world since these whimsical fools dwelt in it.

Then Mrs. Light-mind added as followeth: Come, put this kind of talk away. I was yesterday at Madame Wanton's, where we were as merry as the maids. For who do you think should be there, but I and Mrs. Love-the-flesh, and three or four more, with Mr. Lechery, Mrs. Filth, and some others. So there we had music, and dancing, and what else was meet to fill up the pleasure. And, I dare say, my lady herself is an admirably well-bred gentlewoman, and Mr. Lechery is as pretty a fellow.

By this time, Christiana was got on her way, and Mercy went along with her. So as they went, her children being there also, Christiana began to discourse. And, Mercy, said Christiana, I take this as an unexpected favour, that thou shouldst set foot out of doors with me, to accompany me a little in my way.

MERCY. Then said young Mercy (for she was but young), If I thought it would be to purpose to go with you, I would never go near the town any more.

CHRISTIANA. Well, loving Mercy, I will tell thee what thou shalt do. Go with me to the wicket-gate, and there I will further enquire for thee; and if there thou shalt not meet with encouragement, I will be content that thou shalt return to thy place. I also will pay thee for thy kindness which thou showest to me and my children, in thy accompanying us in our way, as thou dost.

MERCY. Then will I go thither, and will take what shall follow; and the Lord grant that my lot may there fall, even as the King of Heaven shall have his heart upon me.

Christiana then was glad at her heart, not only that she had a companion, but also for that she had prevailed with this poor maid to fall in love with her own salvation. So they went on together, and Mercy began to weep. Then said Christiana, Wherefore weepeth my sister so?

MERCY. Alas! said she, who can but lament, that shall but rightly consider, what a state and condition my poor relations are in that yet remain in our sinful town? and that which makes my grief the more heavy is, because they have no instructor, nor any to tell them what is to come.

CHRISTIANA. Bowels becometh pilgrims; and thou dost for thy friends as my good Christian did for me when he left me; he mourned for that I would not heed nor regard him; but his Lord and ours did gather up his tears and put them into his bottle; and now both I and thou, and these my sweet babes, are reaping the fruit and benefit of them. I hope, Mercy, these tears of thine will not be lost; for the truth hath said, that They that sow in tears shall reap in joy, in singing. And he that goeth forth and weepeth, bearing precious seed, shall doubtless come again with rejoicing, bringing his sheaves with him.

Now my old friend proceeded, and said: But when Christiana came up to the Slough of Dispond, she began to be at a stand; for, said she, this is place in which my dear husband had like to have been smothered with mud. She perceived, also that notwithstanding the command of the King to make this place for pilgrims good, yet it was rather worse than formerly. So I asked if that was true. Yes, said the old gentleman, too true; for that many there be that pretend to be the King's labourers, and that say they are for mending the King's highway, that bring dirt and dung instead of stones, and so mar instead of mending. Here Christiana, therefore, with her boys, did make a stand; but, said Mercy, Come, let us venture, only let us be wary. Then they looked well to the steps, and made a shift to get staggeringly over.

Yet, Christiana had like to have been in, and that not once nor twice. Now they had no sooner got over, but they thought they heard words that said unto them, Blessed is she that believed; for there shall be a performance of those things which were told her from the Lord.

Then they went on again; and said Mercy to Christiana, Had I as good ground to hope for a loving reception at the wicket-gate as you, I think no Slough of Dispond would discourage me.

Well, said the other, you know your sore, and I know mine; and, good friend, we shall all have enough evil before we come at our journey's end.

Thus, now when they had talked away a little more time, they drew nigh to a house which stood in the way, which house was built for the relief of pilgrims; as you will find more fully related in the First Part of these Records of the Pilgrim's Progress. So they drew on towards the house (the House of the Interpreter), and when they came to the door, they heard a great talk in the house. They then gave ear, and heard, as they thought, Christiana mentioned by name. For you must know that there went along, even before her, a talk of her and her children's going on pilgrimage. And this thing was the more pleasing to them, because they had heard that she was Christian's wife, that woman who was sometime ago so unwilling to hear of going on pilgrimage. Thus, therefore, they stood still, and heard the good people within commending her, who, they little thought, stood at the door. At last Christiana knocked, as she had done at the gate before. Now, when she had knocked, there came to the door a young damsel, and opened the door and looked, and behold two women were there.

DAMSEL. Then said the damsel to them, With whom would you speak in this place?

CHRISTIANA. Christiana answered, We understand that this is a privileged place for those that are become pilgrims, and we now at this door are such; wherefore we pray that we may be partakers of that for which we at this time are come; for the day, as thou seest, is very far spent, and we are loath tonight to go any further.

DAMSEL. Pray, what may I call your name, that I may tell it to my Lord within?

CHRISTIANA. My name is Christiana; I was the wife of that pilgrim that some years ago did travel this way, and these be his four children. This maiden also is my companion, and is going on pilgrimage too.

INNOCENT. Then ran Innocent in (for that was her name) and said to those within, Can you think who is at the door? There is Christiana and her children, and her companion, all waiting for entertainment here. Then they leaped for joy, and went and told their master. So he came to the door, and looking upon her, he said, Art thou that Christiana whom Christian, the good man, left behind him, when he betook himself to a pilgrim's life?

CHRISTIANA. I am that woman that was so hard-hearted, as to slight my husband's troubles, and that left him to go on in his journey alone, and these are his four children; but now I also am come, for am I convinced that no way is right but this.

INTERPRETER. Then is fulfilled that which also is written of the man that said to his son, Go, work today in my vineyard. He answered and said, I will not: but afterward he repented and went.

CHRISTIANA. Then said Christiana, So be it, Amen. God make it a true saying upon me, and grant that I may be found at the last of him in peace, without spot, and blameless!

INTERPRETER. But why standest thou thus at the door? Come in, thou daughter of Abraham. We were talking of thee but now, for tidings have come to us before, how thou art become a pilgrim. Come, children, come in; come, maiden, come in. So he had them all into the house.

After a while, because supper was not ready, the Interpreter took them into his significant rooms, and showed them what Christian, Christiana's husband, had seen some time before. Here, therefore, they saw the man in the cage, the man and his dream, the man that cut his way through his enemies, and the picture of the biggest of them all, together with the rest of those things that were then so profitable to Christian.

This done, and after these things had been somewhat digested by Christiana and her company, the Interpreter takes them apart again, and has them first into a room where was a man that could look no way but downwards, with a muck-rake in his hand. There stood also one over his head with a celestial crown in his hand, and proffered him that crown for his muck-rake; but the man did neither look up, nor regard, but raked to himself the straws, the small sticks, and dust of the floor.

Then said Christiana, I persuade myself that I know the meaning of this; for this is a figure of a man of this world, is it not, good Sir?

INTERPRETER. Thou hast said the right, said he, and his muck-rake doth show his carnal mind. And whereas thou seest him rather give heed to rake up straws and sticks, and the dust of the floor, than to what He says that calls to him from above with the celestial crown in his hand, it is to show that heaven is but as a fable to some, and that things here are counted the only things substantial. Now, whereas, it was also showed thee, that the man could look no way but downwards, it is to let thee know that earthly things, when they are with power upon men's minds, quite carry their hearts away from God.

CHRISTIANA. Then said Christiana, O deliver me from this muck-rake!

INTERPRETER. That prayer, said the Interpreter, has lain by till it is almost rusty. Give me not riches, is scarce the prayer of one of ten thousand. Straws, and sticks, and dust, with most, are the great things now looked after.

With that Mercy and Christiana wept, and said, It is, alas! too true.

He had them then into another room, where was a hen and chickens, and bid them observe a while. So one of the chickens went to the trough to drink, and every time she drank, she lift up her head, and her eyes towards heaven. See, said he, what this little chick doth, and learn of her to acknowledge whence your mercies come, by receiving them with looking up. Yet again, said he, observe and look; so they gave heed, and perceived that the hen did talk in a fourfold method towards her chickens. 1. She had a common call, and that she hath all day long. 2. She had a special call, and that she had but sometimes. 3. She had a brooding note. And 4. She had an outcry.

Now, said he, compare this hen to your King, and these chickens to his obedient ones. For, answerable to her, himself has his methods, which he walketh in towards his people; by his common call, he gives nothing; by his special call, he always has something to give; he has also a brooding voice, for them that are under his wing; and he has an outcry, to give the alarm when he seeth the enemy come. I chose, my darlings, to lead you into the room where such things are, because you are women, and they are easy for you.

CHRISTIANA. And Sir, said Christiana, pray let us see some more. So he had them into the slaughter-house, where was a butcher killing of a sheep; and behold the sheep was quiet, and took her death patiently. Then said the Interpreter, You must learn of this sheep to suffer, and to put up wrongs without murmurings and complaints. Behold how quietly she taketh her death, and without objecting, she suffereth her skin to be pulled over her ears. Your King doth call you his sheep.

After this he led them into his garden, where was great variety of flowers; and he said, Do you see all these? So Christiana said, Yes. Then said he again, Behold the flowers are diverse in stature, in quality, and colour, and smell, and virtue; and some are better than some; also where the gardener hath set them, there they stand, and quarrel not with one another.

Again, he had them into his field, which he had sowed with wheat and corn; but when they beheld, the tops of all were cut off, only the straw remained; he said again, This ground was dunged, and ploughed, and sowed; but what shall we do with the crop? Then said Christiana, Burn some, and make muck of the rest. Then said the Interpreter again, Fruit, you see, is that thing you look for, and for want of that you condemn it to the fire, and to be trodden under foot of men: beware that in this you condemn not yourselves.

So, when they were come again into the house, because supper as yet was not ready, Christiana again desired that the Interpreter would either show or tell of some other things that are profitable.

Then the Interpreter began, and said, The fatter the sow is, the more she desires the mire; the fatter the ox is, the more gamesomely he goes to the slaughter; and the more healthy the lusty man is, the more prone he is unto evil.

There is a desire in women to go neat and fine, and it is a comely thing to be adorned with that that in God's sight is of great price.

It is easier watching a night or two, than to sit up a whole year together. So it is easier for one to begin to profess well, than to hold out as he should to the end.

Every shipmaster, when in a storm, will willingly cast that overboard

93

that is of the smallest value in the vessel; but who will throw the best out first? None but he that feareth not God.

One leak will sink a ship; and one sin will destroy a sinner.

He that forgets his friend, is ungrateful unto him; but he that forgets his Saviour, is unmerciful to himself.

He that lives in sin, and looks for happiness hereafter, is like him that soweth cockle, and thinks to fill his barn with wheat or barley.

If a man would live well, let him fetch his last day to him, and make it always his company keeper.

Whispering, and change of thoughts, prove that sin is in the world.

If the world, which God sets light by, is counted a thing of that worth with men; what is heaven, which God commendeth?

If the life that is attended with so many troubles, is so loath to be let go by us, what is the life above?

Everybody will cry up the goodness of men; but who is there that is, as he should, affected with the goodness of God?

We seldom sit down to meat, but we eat and leave; so there is in Jesus Christ more merit and righteousness than the whole world has need of.

Now supper was ready, the table spread, and all things set on the board; so they sat down and did eat, when one had given thanks. And the Interpreter did usually entertain those that lodged with him, with music at meals; so the minstrels played. There was also one that did sing, and a very fine voice he had. His song was this:

> The Lord is only my support,
> And he that doth me feed;
> How can I then want anything
> Whereof I stand in need?

When the song and music was ended, the Interpreter asked Christiana what it was that at first did move her to betake herself to a Pilgrim's life. Christiana answered, First, The loss of my husband came into my mind, at which I was heartily grieved; but all that was but natural affection. Then, after that, came the troubles and pilgrimage of my husband into my mind, and also how like a churl I had carried it to him as to that. So guilt took hold of my mind, and would have drawn me into the pond; but that opportunely I had a dream of the well-being of my husband, and a letter sent me by the King of that country where my husband dwells, to come to him. The dream and the letter together so wrought upon my mind, that they forced me to this way.

The Interpreter then called for a man-servant of his, one Great-heart, and bid him take sword, and helmet, and shield; and take these my daughters, said he, and conduct them to the house called Beautiful, at which place they will rest next. So he took his weapons and went before them; and the Interpreter said, God speed. Those also that belonged to the family, sent them away with many a good wish.

Now I saw in my dream, that they went on, and Great-heart went before them: so they went and came to the place where Christian's burden fell off his back, and tumbled into a sepulchre. Here then they made a pause; and here also they blessed God. Now, said Christiana, it comes to my mind, what was said to us at the gate, to wit, that he should have pardon by word and deed; by word, that is, by the promise; by deed, to wit, in the way it was obtained. What the promise is, of that I know something; but what it is to have pardon by deed, or in the way that it was obtained, Mr. Great-heart, I suppose you know; wherefore, if you please, let us hear you discourse thereof.

GREAT-HEART. Pardon by the deed done, is pardon obtained by some one, for another that hath need thereof: not by the person pardoned, but in the way, saith another, in which I have obtained it. So then, to speak to the question more at large, the pardon that you and Mercy, and these boys have attained, was obtained by another, to wit, by him that let you in at the gate; and he hath obtained it in this double way. He has performed righteousness to cover you, and spilt blood to wash you in.

CHRISTIANA. But if he parts with his righteousness to us, what will he have for himself?

GREAT-HEART. He has more righteousness than you have need of, or than he needeth himself.

CHRISTIANA. Pray make that appear.

GREAT-HEART. With all my heart; but first I must premise, that he of whom we are now about to speak is one that has not his fellow. He has two natures in one person, plain to be distinguished, impossible to be divided. Unto each of these natures a righteousness belongeth, and each righteousness is essential to that nature; so that one may as easily cause the nature to be extinct, as to separate its justice or righteousness from it. Of these righteousnesses, therefore, we are not made partakers, so as that they, or any of them, should be put upon us, that we might be made just, and live thereby. Besides these, there is a righteousness which this Person has, as these two natures are joined in one: and this is not the righteousness of the Godhead, as distinguished from the manhood; nor the righteousness of the manhood, as distinguished from the Godhead; but a righteousness which standeth in the union of both natures, and may properly be called, the righteousness that is essential to his being prepared of God to the capacity of the mediatory office, which he was to be entrusted with.

CHRISTIANA. But are the other righteousnesses of no use to us?

GREAT-HEART. Yes; for though they are essential to his natures and office, and so cannot be communicated unto another, yet it is by virtue of them, that the righteousness that justifies, is, for that purpose, efficacious. The righteousness of his Godhead gives virtue to his obedience; the righteousness of his manhood giveth capability to his obedience to justify; and the righteousness that standeth in the union of these two natures to his office, giveth authority to that righteousness to do the work for which it is ordained.

So then, here is a righteousness that Christ, as God, has no need of, for he is God without it; here is a righteousness that Christ, as man, has no need of to make him so, for he is perfect man without it; again, here is a righteousness that Christ, as God-man, has no need of, for he is perfectly so without it. Here, then, is a righteousness that Christ, as God, as man, as God-man, has no need of, with reference to himself, and therefore he can spare it; a justifying righteousness, that he for himself wanteth not, and therefore he giveth it away; hence it is called the gift of righteousness. This righteousness, since Christ Jesus the Lord has made himself under the law, must be given away; for the law doth not only bind him that is under it to do justly, but to use charity. Wherefore he must, he ought, by the law, if he hath two coats, to give one to him that hath none. Now, our Lord, indeed, hath two coats, one for himself, and one to spare; wherefore he freely bestows one upon those that have none. And thus, Christiana, and Mercy, and the rest of you that are here, doth your pardon come by deed, or by the work of another man. Your Lord Christ is he that has worked, and has given away what he wrought for, to the next poor beggar he meets.

But, again, in order to pardon by deed, there must something be paid to God as a price, as well as something prepared to cover us withal. Sin has delivered us up to the just curse of a righteous law; now, from this curse we must be justified by way of redemption, a price being paid for the harms we have done; and this is by the blood of your Lord, who came and stood in your place and stead, and died your death for your transgressions. Thus has he ransomed you from your transgressions by blood, and covered your polluted and deformed souls with righteousness. For the sake of which, God passeth by you, and will not hurt you, when he comes to judge the world.

CHRISTIANA. This is brave. Now, I see there was something to be learned by our being pardoned by word and deed. Good Mercy, let us labour to keep this in mind; and my children, do you remember it also. But, Sir, was not this it that made my good Christian's burden fall from off his shoulder and that made him give three leaps for joy?

GREAT-HEART. Yes, it was the belief of this, that cut those strings, that could not be cut by other means; and it was to give him a proof of the virtue of this, that he was suffered to carry his burden to the cross.

CHRISTIANA. I thought so; for though my heart was lightful and joyous before, yet it is ten times more lightsome and joyous now. And I am persuaded by what I have felt, though I have felt but little as yet, that if the most burdened man in the world was here, and did see and believe as I now do, it would make his heart the more merry and blithe.

GREAT-HEART. There is not only comfort, and the ease of a burden brought to us, by the sight and consideration of these, but an endeared affection begot in us by it; for who can, if he doth but once think that pardon comes not only by promise, but thus, but be affected with the way and means of his redemption, and so, with the man that hath wrought it for him?

96

CHRISTIANA. True; methinks it makes my heart bleed to think that he should bleed for me. O thou loving One! O thou blessed One! Thou deservest to have me; thou hast bought me; thou deservest to have me all; thou hast paid for me ten thousand times more than I am worth! No marvel that this made the water stand in my husband's eyes, and that it made him trudge so nimbly on; I am persuaded he wished me with him; but, vile wretch that I was, I let him come all alone. O Mercy, that thy father and mother were here; yea, and Mrs. Timorous also; nay, I wish now with all my heart, that here was Madam Wanton too. Surely, surely their hearts would be affected; nor could the fear of the one, nor the powerful lusts of the other, prevail with them to go home again, and to refuse to become good pilgrims.

GREAT-HEART. You speak now in the warmth of your affections. Will it, think you, be always thus with you? Besides, this is not communicated to every one that did see your Jesus bleed. There were that stood by, and that saw the blood run from his heart to the ground, and yet were so far off this, that, instead of lamenting, they laughed at him; and, instead of becoming his disciples, did harden their hearts against him. So that all that you have, my daughters, you have by a peculiar impression made by a Divine contemplating upon what I have spoken to you. Remember that it was told you, that the hen, by her common call, gives no meat to her chickens. This you have, therefore, by a special grace.

Now, I saw still in my dream, that they went on until they were come to the place that Simple, and Sloth, and Presumption, lay and slept in, when Christian went by on pilgrimage; and, behold, they were hanged up in irons a little way off on the other side.

MERCY. Then said Mercy to him that was their guide and conductor, What are those three men? and for what are they hanged there?

GREAT-HEART. These three men were men of very bad qualities. They had no mind to be pilgrims themselves, and whosoever they could they hindered. They were for sloth and folly themselves, and whoever they could persuade with, they made so too; and, withal, taught them to presume that they should do well at last. They were asleep when Christian went by; and now you go by, they are hanged.

Thus they went on, till they came at the foot of the Hill Difficulty, where, again, their good friend, Mr. Great-heart, took an occasion to tell them of what happened there when Christian himself went by. So he had them first to the spring. Lo, said he, this is the spring that Christian drank of, before he went up this hill; and then it was clear and good, but now it is dirty with the feet of some that are not desirous that pilgrims here should quench their thirst. Threat Mercy said, And why so envious, trow? But, said their guide, it will do, if taken up, and put into a vessel that is sweet and good; for then the dirt will sink to the bottom, and the water come out by itself more clear. Thus, therefore, Christiana and her companions were compelled to do. They took it up, and put it into an earthen pot, and so let it stand till the dirt was gone to the bottom, and then they drank thereof.

Next, he showed them the two by-ways that were at the foot of the hill, where Formality and Hypocrisy lost themselves. And, said he, these are dangerous paths. Two were here cast away when Christian came by. And although, as you see, these ways are since stopped up with chains, posts, and a ditch, yet there are that will choose to adventure here, rather than take the pains to go up this hill.

When they had passed by this place, they came upon the borders of the Shadow of Death; a place, also, most strangely haunted with evil things, as many are able to testify; but these women and children went the better through it, because they had daylight, and because Mr. Great-heart was their conductor.

When they were entered upon this Valley, they thought that they heard a groaning, as of dead men, a very great groaning. They thought, also, they did hear words of lamentation spoken, as of some in extreme torment. These things made the boys to quake, the women also looked pale and wan; but their guide bid them be of good comfort.

So they went on a little farther, and they thought that they felt the ground begin to shake under them, as if some hollow place was there; they heard also a kind of a hissing, as of serpents, but nothing as yet appeared. Then said the boys, Are we not yet at the end of this doleful place? But the guide also bid them be of good courage, and look well to their feet, lest haply, said he, you be taken in some snare.

Now James began to be sick, but I think the cause thereof was fear; so his mother gave him some of that glass of spirits that she had given her at the Interpreter's house, and three of the pills that Mr. Skill had prepared, and the boy began to revive. Thus they went on, till they came to about the middle of the Valley, and then Christiana said, Methinks I see something yonder upon the road before us, a thing of such a shape such as I have not seen. Then said Joseph, Mother, what is it? An ugly thing, child; an ugly thing, said she. But, mother, what is it like? said he. It is like I cannot tell what, said she. And now it was but a little way off; then said she, It is nigh.

Well, well, said Mr. Great-heart, let them that are most afraid, keep close to me. So the fiend came on, and the conductor met it; but when it was just come to him, it vanished to all their sights. Then remembered they what had been said some time ago, Resist the devil, and he will flee from you.

They went therefore on, as being a little refreshed; but they had not gone far, before Mercy, looking behind her, saw, as she thought, something most like a lion, and it came a great padding pace after; and it had a hollow voice of roaring; and at every roar that it gave, it made all the Valley echo, and their hearts to ache, save the heart of him that was their guide. So it came up; and Mr. Great-heart went behind, and put the Pilgrims all before him. The lion also came on apace, and Mr. Great-heart addressed himself to give him battle. But when he saw that it was determined that resistance should be made, he also drew back, and came no farther.

Then they went on again, and their conductor did go before them, till they came at a place where was cast up a pit the whole breadth of the way; and, before they could be prepared to go over that, a great mist and a darkness fell upon them, so that they could not see. Then said the Pilgrims, Alas! now what shall we do? But their guide made answer, Fear not, stand still, and see what an end will be put to this also. So they staid there, because their path was marred. They then also thought that they did hear more apparently the noise and rushing of the enemies; the fire, also, and the smoke of the pit, was much easier to be discerned. Then said Christiana to Mercy, Now I see what my poor husband went through; I have heard much of this place, but I never was here before now. Poor man, he went here all alone in the night; he had night almost quite through the way; also, these fiends were busy about him, as if they would have torn him in pieces. Many have spoke of it, but none can tell what the Valley of the Shadow of Death should mean, until they come in it themselves The heart knows its own bitterness; and a stranger intermeddleth not with its joy. To be here is a fearful thing.

So they cried and prayed, and God sent light and deliverance, for there was now no let in their way; no not there, where but now they were stopped with a pit. Yet they were not got through the Valley; so they went on still, and behold great stinks and loathsome smells, to the great annoyance of them. Then said Mercy to Christiana, There is not such pleasant being here, as at the gate, or at the Interpreter's, or at the house where we lay last.

O but, said one of the boys, it is not so bad to go through here, as it is to abide here always; and for aught I know, one reason why we must go this way to the house prepared for us, is, that our home might be made the sweeter to us.

Well said, Samuel, quoth the guide, thou hast now spoke like a man. Why, if ever I get out here again, said the boy, I think I shall prize light and good way better than ever I did in all my life. Then said the guide, We shall be out by and by.

So on they went, and Joseph said, Cannot we see to the end of this Valley as yet? Then said the guide, Look to your feet, for you shall presently be among the snares. So they looked to their feet, and went on; but they were troubled much with the snares. Now, when they were come among the snares, they espied a man cast into the ditch on the left hand, with his flesh all rent and torn. Then said the guide, That is one Heedless, that was a-going this way; he has lain there a great while. There was one Take-heed with him, when he was taken and slain; but he escaped their hands. You cannot imagine how many are killed hereabout, and yet men are so foolishly venturous, as to set out lightly on pilgrimage, and to come without a guide. Poor Christian! it was a wonder that he here escaped; but he was beloved of his God: also, he had a good heart of his own, or else he could never have done it. Now they drew towards the end of the way; and just there where Christian had seen the cave when he went by, out

99

thence came forth Maul, a giant. This Maul did use to spoil young pilgrims with sophistry; and he called Great-heart by his name, and said unto him, How many times have you been forbidden to do these things? Then said Mr. Great-heart, What things? What things? quoth the giant; you know what things; but I will put an end to your trade. But pray, said Mr. Great-heart, before we fall to it, let us understand wherefore we must fight. Now the women and children stood trembling, and knew not what to do. Quoth the giant, You rob the country, and rob it with the worst of thefts. These are but generals, said Mr. Great-heart; come to particulars, man.

Then said the giant, Thou practisest the craft of a kidnapper; thou gatherest up women and children, and carriest them into a strange country, to the weakening of my master's kingdom. But now Great-heart replied, I am a servant of the God of heaven; my business is to persuade sinners to repentance; I am commanded to do my endeavour to turn men, women, and children, from darkness to light, and from the power of Satan unto God; and if this be indeed the ground of thy quarrel, let us fall to it as soon as thou wilt.

Then the giant came up, and Mr. Great-heart went to meet him; and as he went, he drew his sword, but the giant had a club. So without more ado, they fell to it, and at the first blow the giant struck Mr. Great-heart down upon one of his knees; with that the women and children cried out; so Mr. Great-heart recovering himself, said about him in full lusty manner, and gave the giant a wound in his arm; thus he fought for the space of an hour, to that height of heat, that the breath came out of the giant's nostrils, as the heat doth out of a boiling cauldron.

Then they sat down to rest them, but Mr. Great-heart betook him to prayer; also the women and children did nothing but sigh and cry all the time that the battle did last.

When they had rested them, and taken breath, they both fell to it again, and Mr. Great-heart with a full blow, fetched the giant down to the ground. Nay, hold, and let me recover, quoth he; so Mr. Great-heart fairly let him get up. So to it they went again, and the giant missed but little of all to breaking Mr. Great-heart's skull with his club.

Mr. Great-heart seeing that, runs to him in the full heat of his spirit, and pierceth him under the fifth rib; with that the giant began to faint, and could hold up his club no longer. Then Mr. Great-heart seconded his blow, and smote the head of the giant from his shoulders. Then the women and children rejoiced, and Mr. Great-heart also praised God, for the deliverance he had wrought.

When this was done, they among them erected a pillar, and fastened the giant's head thereon, and wrote underneath in letters, that passengers might read:

> He that did wear this head, was one
> That pilgrims did misuse;
> He stopp'd their way, he spared none,
> But did them all abuse;

Until that I, Great-heart, arose,
The pilgrim's guide to be;
Until that I did him oppose,
That was their enemy.

Now I saw, that they went to the ascent that was a little way off, cast up to be a prospect for pilgrims (that was the place from whence Christian had the first sight of Faithful his brother); wherefore here they sat down, and rested; they also here did eat and drink, and make merry, for that they had gotten deliverance from this so dangerous an enemy. As they sat thus, and did eat, Christiana asked the guide if he had caught no hurt in the battle. Then said Mr. Great-heart, No, save a little on my flesh; yet that also shall be so far from being to my detriment, that it is at present a proof of my love to my Master and you, and shall be a means, by grace, to increase my reward at last.

Then they got up and went forward. Now a little before them stood an oak; and under it, when they came to it, they found an old pilgrim fast asleep; they knew that he was a pilgrim by his clothes, and his staff, and his girdle.

So the guide, Mr. Great-heart, awakened him, and the old gentleman, as he lift up his eyes, cried out, What's the matter? Who are you? and what is your business here?

GREAT-HEART. Come, man, be not so hot, here is none but friends; yet the old man gets up, and stands upon his guard, and will know of them what they were. Then said the guide, My name is Great-heart; I am the guide of these Pilgrims, which are going to the Celestial Country.

HONEST. Then said Mr. Honest, I cry you mercy; I feared that you had been of the company of those that some time ago did rob Little-faith of his money; but now I look better about me, I perceive you are honester people.

GREAT-HEART. Why, what would, or could you have done, to have helped yourself, if we indeed had been of that company.

HONEST. Done! why I would have fought as long as breath had been in me; and had I so done, I am sure you could never have given me the worst on it; for a Christian can never be overcome, unless he should yield of himself.

GREAT-HEART. Well said, father Honest, quoth the guide; for by this I know thou art a cock of the right kind, for thou hast said the truth.

HONEST. And by this, also, I know that thou knowest what true pilgrimage is; for all others do think that we are the soonest overcome of any.

GREAT-HEART. Well, now we are so happily met, pray let me crave your name, and the name of the place you came from.

HONEST. My name I cannot; but I came from the town of Stupidity; it lieth about four degrees beyond the City of Destruction.

GREAT-HEART. Oh! are you that countryman, then? I deem I have half a guess of you; your name is Old Honesty, is it not? So the old gentleman

101

blushed, and said, Not Honesty, in the abstract, but Honest is my name; and I wish that my nature shall agree to what I am called.

HONEST. But, Sir, said the old gentleman, how could you guess that I am such a man, since I came from such a place?

GREAT-HEART. I had heard of you before, by my Master; for he knows all things that are done on the earth; but I have often wondered that any should come from your place, for your town is worse than is the City of Destruction itself.

HONEST. Yes, we lie more off from the sun, and so are more cold and senseless; but was a man in a mountain of ice, yet if the Sun of Righteousness will arise upon him, his frozen heart shall feel a thaw; and thus it hath been with me.

GREAT-HEART. I believe it, father Honest, I believe it; for I know the thing is true.

Then the old gentleman saluted all the Pilgrims with a holy kiss of charity; and asked of them their names, and how they had fared since they set out on their pilgrimage.

CHRISTIANA. Then said Christiana, My name, I suppose you have heard of; good Christian was my husband, and these four were his children. But can you think how the old gentleman was taken, when she told him who she was! He skipped, he smiled, and blessed them with a thousand good wishes, saying:

HONEST. I have heard much of your husband, and of his travels and wars, which he underwent in his days. Be it spoken to your comfort, the name of your husband rings over all these parts of the world: his faith, his courage, his enduring, and his sincerity under all, have made his name famous.

Christiana then wished for an inn for herself and the children because they were weary. Then said Mr. Honest there is one a little before us where a very honourable disciple, one Gaius, dwells. So they went thither and stayed there that night. Next morning Gaius came to them.

Well, said Gaius, since, as I know, Mr. Great-heart is good at his weapons, if you please, after we have refreshed ourselves, we will walk into the fields, to see if we can do any good. About a mile from hence, there is one Slay-good, a giant that does much annoy the King's highway in these parts; and I know whereabout his haunt is. He is master of a number of thieves; it would be well if we could clear these parts of him.

So they consented, and went, Mr. Great-heart with his sword, helmet, and shield, and the rest with spears and staves.

When they came to the place where he was, they found him with one Feeble-mind in his hands, whom his servants had brought unto him, having taken him in the way. Now the giant was rifling him, with a purpose, after that, to pick his bones, for he was of the nature of flesh-eaters.

Well, so soon as he saw Mr. Great-heart and his friends at the mouth of his cave with their weapons, he demanded what they wanted.

GREAT-HEART. We want thee; for we are come to revenge the quarrel of the many that thou hast slain of the pilgrims, when thou hast dragged them out of the King's highway; wherefore, come out of thy cave. So he armed himself and came out; and to a battle they went, and fought for above an hour, and then stood still to take wind.

SLAY-GOOD. Then said the giant, Why are you here on my ground?

GREAT-HEART. To revenge the blood of pilgrims, as I also told thee before. So they went to it again, and the giant made Mr. Great-heart give back; but he came up again, and, in the greatness of his mind, he let fly with such stoutness at the giant's head and sides, that he made him let his weapon fall out of his hand; so he smote him, and slew him, and cut off his head, and brought it away to the inn. He also took Feeble-mind, the pilgrim, and brought him with him to his lodgings. When they were come home, they showed his head to the family, and then set it up, as they had done others before, for a terror to those that shall attempt to do as he hereafter.

GAIUS. Come, Sir, said good Gaius, be of good cheer, you are welcome to me, and to my house, and that thou hast a mind to, call for freely; and what thou wouldest have my servants do for thee, they will do it with a ready mind.

Then said Mr. Feeble-mind, This is unexpected favour, and as the sun shining out of a very dark cloud. Did Giant Slay-good intend me this favour when he stopped me, and resolved to let me go no further? Did he intend, that after he had rifled my pockets, I should go to Gaius, mine host? Yet so it is.

Now, just as Mr. Feeble-mind and Gaius were thus in talk, there comes one running, and called at the door, and told that, about a mile and a half off, there was one Mr. Not-right, a pilgrim, struck dead upon the place where he was with a thunder-bolt.

FEEBLE-MIND. Alas! said Mr. Feeble-mind, is he slain? He overtook me some days before I came so far as hither, and would be my company-keeper. He also was with me when Slay-good, the giant, took me; but he was nimble of his heels, and escaped. But, it seems, he escaped to die, and I was took to live.

What, one would think, doth seek to slay outright,
Oft-times delivers from the saddest plight.
That very providence, whose face is death,
Doth oft-times to the lowly life bequeath.
I taken was, he did escape and flee;
Hands cross'd gives death to him, and life to me.

Now, about this time, Matthew and Mercy were married. Also Gaius gave his daughter Phebe to James, Matthew's brother, to wife; after which time they yet staid above ten days at Gaius's house, spending their time, and the seasons, like as pilgrims used to do.

When they were to depart, Gaius made them a feast, and they did eat and drink, and were merry. Now the hour was come that they must be gone; wherefore, Mr. Great-heart called for a reckoning; but Gaius told him, that at his house it was not the custom for pilgrims to pay for their entertainment. He boarded them by the year, but looked for his pay from the good Samaritan, who had promised him, at his return, whatsoever charge he was at with them, faithfully, to repay him. Then said Mr. Great-heart to him,

GREAT-HEART. Beloved, thou dost faithfully whatsoever thou dost to the brethren, and to strangers; which have borne witness of thy charity before the church; whom if thou (yet) bring forward on their journey after a godly sort, thou shalt do well.

Then Gaius took his leave of them all, and of his children, and particularly of Mr. Feeble-mind. He also gave him something to drink by the way.

Now Mr. Feeble-mind, when they were going out of the door, made as if he intended to linger; the which when Mr. Great-heart espied, he said, Come, Mr. Feeble-mind, pray do you go along with us, I will be your conductor, and you shall fare as the rest.

FEEBLE-MIND. Alas! I want a suitable companion; you are all lusty and strong; but I, as you see, am weak; I chuse, therefore, rather to come behind, lest, by reason of my many infirmities, I should be both a burden to myself and to you.

GREAT-HEART. But, brother, said Mr. Great-heart, I have it in commission to comfort the feeble-minded, and to support the weak. You must needs go along with us; we will wait for you; we will lend you our help; we will deny ourselves of some things, both opinionative and practical, for your sake, we will not enter into doubtful disputations before you; we will be made all things to you, rather than you shall be left behind.

Now all this while they were at Gaius's door; and behold, as they were thus in the heat of their discourse, Mr. Ready-to-halt came by, with his crutches in his hand; and he also was going on pilgrimage.

FEEBLE-MIND. Then said Mr. Feeble-mind to him. Man, how camest thou hither? I was but just now complaining, that I had not a suitable companion, but thou art according to my wish. Welcome, welcome, good Mr. Ready-to-halt, I hope thee and I may be some help.

READY-TO-HALT. I shall be glad of thy company, said the other; and good Mr. Feeble-mind, rather than we will part, since we are thus happily met, I will lend thee one of my crutches.

FEEBLE-MIND. Nay, said he, though I thank thee for thy goodwill, I am not inclined to halt before I am lame. Howbeit, I think, when occasion is, it may help me against a dog.

READY-TO-HALT. If either myself or my crutches can do thee a pleasure, we are both at thy command, good Mr. Feeblemind.

Thus therefore they went on; Mr. Great-heart and Mr. Honest went before, Christiana and her children went next, and Mr. Feeble-mind and Mr. Ready-to-halt, came behind with his crutches. Then said Mr. Honest,

HONEST. Pray, Sir, now we are upon the road, tell us some profitable things of some that have gone on pilgrimage before us.

GREAT-HEART. With a good will. I suppose you have heard how Chris-

104

tian of old did meet with Apollyon in the Valley of Humiliation; and also what hard work he had, to go through the Valley of the Shadow of Death. Also I think you cannot but have heard how Faithful was put to it with Madam Wanton, with Adam the first, with one Discontent, and Shame, four as deceitful villains as a man can meet with upon the road.

HONEST. Yes, I have heard of all this; but indeed, good Faithful was hardest put to it with Shame; he was an unwearied one.

GREAT-HEART. Aye; for, as the Pilgrim well said, he of all men had the wrong name.

HONEST. But pray, Sir, where was it that Christian and Faithful met Talkative? That same was also a notable one.

GREAT-HEART. He was a confident fool, yet many follow his ways.

HONEST. He had like to have beguiled Faithful.

GREAT-HEART. Aye, but Christian put him into a way quickly to find him out. Thus they went on till they came at the place where Evangelist met with Christian and Faithful, and prophesied to them of what should befall them at Vanity Fair.

GREAT-HEART. Then said their guide, Hereabouts did Christian and Faithful meet with Evangelist, who prophesied to them of what troubles they should meet with at Vanity Fair.

HONEST. Say you so? I dare say it was a hard chapter that then he did read unto them.

GREAT-HEART. It was so; but he gave them encouragement withal. But what do we talk of them? they were a couple of lion-like men; they had set their faces like flint. Don't you remember how undaunted they were when they stood before the judge?

HONEST. Well, Faithful bravely suffered.

GREAT-HEART. So he did, and as brave things came on it; for Hopeful and some others, as the story relates it, were converted by his death.

Now, by this time, they were come within sight of the town of Vanity, where Vanity Fair is kept. So, when they saw that they were so near the town, they consulted with one another, how they should pass through the town; and some said one thing, and some another. At last Mr. Great-heart said, I have, as you may understand, often been a conductor of pilgrims through this town; now I am acquainted with one Mr. Mnason, a Cyprusian by nation, and old disciple, at whose house we may lodge. If you think good, said he, we will turn in there.

Content, said old Honest; Content, said Christiana; Content, said Mr. Feeble-mind; and so they said all. Now, you must think, it was even-tide by that they got to the outside of the town; but Mr. Great-heart knew the way to the old man's house. So thither they came; and he called at the door, and the old man within knew his tongue so soon as ever he heard it; so he opened, and they all came in. Then said Mnason their host, How far have ye come today? So they said, From the house of Gaius our friend. I promise you, said he, you have gone a good stitch, you may well be a-weary; sit down. So they sat down.

GREAT-HEART. Then said their guide, Come, what cheer, Sirs? I dare say you are welcome to my friend.

MNASON. I also, said Mr. Mnason, do bid you welcome, and, whatever you want, do but say, and we will do what we can to get it for you.

HONEST. Our great want, a while since, was harbour and good company, and now I hope we have both.

MNASON. For harbour, you see what it is; but for good company, that will appear in the trial.

GREAT-HEART. Well, said Mr. Great-heart, will you have the Pilgrims up into their lodging?

MNASON. I will, said Mr. Mnason. So he had them to their respective places; and also showed them a very fair dining-room, where they might be, and sup together, until time was come to go to rest.

Now, when they were set in their places, and were a little cheery after their journey, Mr. Honest asked his landlord, if there were any store of good people in the town?

MNASON. We have a few, for indeed they are but a few, when compared with them on the other side.

HONEST. But how shall we do to see some of them? for the sight of good men to them that are going on pilgrimage, is like to the appearing of the moon and the stars to them that are sailing upon the seas.

Then Mr. Mnason stamped with his foot, and his daughter Grace came up; so he said unto her, Grace, go you, tell my friends, Mr. Contrite, Mr. Holy-man, Mr. Love-saint, Mr. Dare-not-lye, and Mr. Penitent, that I have a friend or two at my house that have a mind this evening to see them.

So Grace went to call them, and they came; and, after salutation made, they sat down together at the table.

HONEST. Then Mr. Honest (when they were all sat down) asked Mr. Contrite, and the rest, in what posture their town was at present?

CONTRITE. You may be sure we are full of hurry in fair-time. It is hard keeping our hearts and spirits in any good order, when we are in a cumbered condition. He that lives in such a place as this is, and that has to do with such such as we have, has need of an item, to caution him to take heed, every moment of the day.

HONEST. But how are your neighbours for quietness?

CONTRITE. They are much more moderate now than formerly. You know how Christian and Faithful were used at our town; but of late, I say, they have been far more moderate. I think the blood of Faithful lieth with load upon them till now; for since they burned him, they have been ashamed to burn any more. In those days we were afraid to walk the streets, but now we can show our heads. Then the name of a professor was odious; now, especially in some parts of our town (for you know our town is large), religion is counted honourable.

Then said Mr. Contrite to them, Pray how fareth it with you in your pilgrimage? How stands the country affected towards you?

HONEST. It happens to us as it happeneth to way-faring men; sometimes our way is clean, sometimes foul, sometimes up hill, sometimes down hill; we are seldom at a certainty; the wind is not always on our backs, nor is every one a friend that we meet with in the way. We have met with some notable rubs already; and what are yet behind, we know not; but for the most part, we find it true, that has been talked of, of old, A good man must suffer trouble.

CONTRITE. You talk of rubs; what rubs have you met withal?

HONEST. Nay, ask Mr. Great-heart, our guide, for he can give the best account of that.

GREAT-HEART. We have been beset three or four times already. First, Christiana and her children were beset with two ruffians, that they feared would a took away their lives. We were beset with Giant Bloody-man, Giant Maul, and Giant Slay-good. Indeed we did rather beset the last, than were beset of him. And thus it was: After we had been some time at the house of Gaius, mine host, and of the whole church, we were minded upon a time to take our weapons with us, and so go see if we could light upon any of those that were enemies to pilgrims (for we heard that there was a notable one thereabouts). Now Gaius knew his haunt better than I, because he dwelt thereabout; so we looked, and looked, till at last we discerned the mouth of his cave; then we were glad, and plucked up our spirits. So we approached up to his den, and lo, when we came there, he had dragged, by mere force, into his net, this poor man, Mr. Feeble-mind, and was about to bring him to his end. But when he saw us, supposing, as we thought, he had had another prey, he left the poor man in his hole, and came out. So we fell to it full sore, and he lustily laid about him; but in conclusion, he was brought down to the ground, and his head cut off, and set up by the way-side, for a terror to such as should after practise such ungodliness. That I tell you the truth, here is the man himself to affirm it, who was as a lamb taken out of the mouth of the lion.

FEEBLE-MIND. Then said Mr. Feeble-mind, I found this true, to my cost, and comfort; to my cost, when he threatened to pick my bones every moment; and to my comfort, when I saw Mr. Great-heart and his friends with their weapons, approach so near for my deliverance.

HOLY-MAN. Then said Mr. Holy-man, There are two things that they have need to be possessed with, that go on pilgrimage; courage, and an unspotted life. If they have not courage, they can never hold on their way; and if their lives be loose, they will make the very name of a pilgrim stink.

LOVE-SAINT. Then said Mr. Love-saint, I hope this caution is not needful amongst you. But truly, there are many that go upon the road, that rather declare themselves strangers to pilgrimage, than strangers and pilgrims in the earth.

DARE-NOT-LYE. Then said Mr. Dare-not-lye, It is true, they neither have the pilgrim's weed, nor the pilgrim's courage; they go not uprightly, but all awry with their feet; one shoe goes inward, another outward, and their hosen out behind; there a rag, and there a rent, to the disparagement of their Lord.

PENITENT. These things, said Mr. Penitent, they ought to be troubled for; nor are the pilgrims like to have that grace put upon them and their pilgrim's progress, as they desire, until the way is cleared of such spots and blemishes.

Thus they sat talking and spending the time, until supper was set upon the table; unto which they went and refreshed their weary bodies; so they went to rest. Now they stayed in this fair a great while, at the house of this Mr. Mnason, who, in process of time, gave his daughter Grace unto Samuel, Christiana's son, to wife, and his daughter Martha to Joseph.

While they lay here, there came a monster out of the woods, and slew many of the people of the town. It would also carry away their children, and teach them to suck its whelps. Now, no man in the town durst so much as face this monster; but all men fled when they heard of the noise of his coming.

The monster was like unto no one beast upon the earth; its body was like a dragon, and it had seven heads and ten horns. It made great havoc of children, and yet it was governed by a woman. This monster propounded conditions to men, and such men as loved their lives more than their souls, accepted of those conditions. So they came under.

Now this Mr. Great-heart, together with these that came to visit the pilgrims at Mr. Mnason's house, entered into a covenant to go and engage this beast, if perhaps they might deliver the people of this town from the paws and mouth of this so devouring a serpent.

The monster, you must know, had his certain seasons to come out in, and to make his attempts upon the children of the people of the town; also these seasons did these valiant worthies watch him in, and did still continually assault him; insomuch, that in process of time he became not only wounded, but lame; also he has not made that havoc of the townsmen's children, as formerly he has done. And it is verily believed by some, that this beast will die of his wounds.

Well, the time grew on that the Pilgrims must go on their way, wherefore they prepared for their journey. They sent for their friends; they conferred with them; they had some time set apart, therein to commit each other to the protection of their Prince. There were again, that brought them of such things as they had, that were fit for the weak and the strong, for the women and the men, and so laded them with such things as were necessary.

They, therefore, that were of the Pilgrims' company went on, and Mr. Great-heart went before them. Now the women and children being weakly, they were forced to go as they could bear; by this means Mr. Ready-to-halt and Mr. Feeble-mind had more to sympathize with their condition.

When they were gone from the townsmen, and when their friends had bid them farewell; they quickly came to the place where Faithful was put to death; there therefore they made a stand, and thanked Him that had enabled him to bear his cross so well; and the rather because they now found that they had a benefit by such a manly suffering as his was.

They went on, therefore, after this, a good way farther, talking of Chris-

108

tian and Faithful; and how Hopeful joined himself to Christian after that Faithful was dead.

I saw now that they went on, till they came at the river that was on this side of the Delectable Mountains. To the river where the fine trees grow on both sides; and whose leaves, if taken inwardly, are good against surfeits, where the meadows are green all the year long, and where they might lie down safely.

By this river side, in the meadow, there were cotes and folds for sheep, a house built for the nourishing and bringing up of those lambs, the babes of those women that go on pilgrimage. Also there was here one that was entrusted with them, who could have compassion, and that could gather these lambs with his arms, and carry them in his bosom, and that could gently lead those that were with young. Now to the care of this man, Christiana admonished her four daughters to commit their little ones, that by these waters they might be housed, harboured, succoured, and nourished, and that none of them might be lacking in time to come. This man, if any of them go astray, or be lost, he will bring them again; he will also bind up that which was broken, and will strengthen them that are sick. Here they will never want meat, and drink, and clothing; here they will be kept from thieves and robbers; for this man will die before one of those committed to his trust shall be lost. Besides, here they shall be sure to have good nurture and admonition, and shall be taught to walk in right paths, and that you know is a favour of no small account. Also here, as you see, are delicate waters, pleasant meadows, dainty flowers, variety of trees, and such as bear wholesome fruit; fruit not like that that Matthew ate of, that fell over the wall out of Beelzebub's garden; but fruit that procureth health where there is none, and that continueth and increaseth it where it is.

So they were content to commit their little ones to him; and that which was also an encouragement to them so to do, was, for that all this was to be at the charge of the King, and so was an hospital for young children and orphans.

Now they went on; and when they were come to By-path Meadow, to the stile over which Christian went with his fellow Hopeful, when they were taken by Giant Despair, and put into Doubting Castle; they sat down and consulted what was best to be done; to wit, now they were so strong, and had got such a man as Mr. Great-heart for their conductor, whether they had not best to make an attempt upon the Giant, demolish his castle, and, if there were any pilgrims in it, to set them at liberty, before they went any farther. So one said one thing, and another said the contrary. One questioned if it was lawful to go upon unconsecrated ground; another said they might, provided their end was good; but Mr. Great-heart said, Though that assertion offered last cannot be universally true, yet I have a commandment to resist sin, to overcome evil, to fight the good fight of faith; and, I pray, with whom should I fight this good fight, if not with Giant Despair? I will, therefore, attempt the taking away of his life, and the demolishing of Doubting Castle. Then said he, Who will go with me?

Then said old Honest, I will. And so will we too, said Christiana's four sons, Matthew, Samuel, James, and Joseph; for they were young men and strong. So they left the women in the road, and with them Mr. Feeble-mind and Mr. Ready-to-halt with his crutches, to be their guard, until they came back; for in that place though Giant Despair dwelt so near, they keeping in the road, a little child might lead them.

So Mr. Great-heart, old Honest, and the four young men, went to go up to Doubting Castle, to look for Giant Despair. When they came at the Castle-gate, they knocked for entrance with an unusual noise. At that the old Giant comes to the gate, and Diffidence, his wife, follows. Then said he, Who, and what is he that is so hardy, as after this manner to molest the Giant Despair? Mr. Great-heart replied, It is I, Great-heart, one of the King of the Celestial Country's conductors of pilgrims to their place; and I demand of thee that thou open thy gates for my entrance. Prepare thyself also to fight, for I am come to take away thy head, and to demolish Doubting Castle.

Now Giant Despair, because he was a giant, thought no man could overcome him; and, again, thought he, since heretofore. I have made a conquest of angels, shall Great-heart make me afraid! So he harnessed himself, and went out. He had a cap of steel upon his head, a breast-plate of fire girded to him, and he came out in iron shoes with a great club in his hand. Then these six men made up to him, and beset him behind and before. Also when Diffidence, the giantess, came up to help him, old Mr. Honest cut her down at one blow. Then they fought for their lives, and Giant Despair was brought down to the ground, but was very loath to die. He struggled hard, and had, as they say, as many lives as a cat; but Great-heart was his death, for he left him not till he had severed his head from his shoulders.

Then they fell to demolishing Doubting Castle, and that you know might with ease be done, since Giant Despair was dead. They were seven days in destroying of that; and in it of pilgrims they found one Mr. Dispondency, almost starved to death, and one Much-afraid, his daughter; these two they saved alive. But it would have made you a-wondered to have seen the dead bodies that lay here and there in these castle-yard, and how full of dead men's bones the dungeon was.

When Mr. Great-heart and his companions had performed this exploit, they took Mr. Dispondency, and his daughter Much-afraid, into their protection; for they were honest people, though they were prisoners in Doubting Castle, to that tyrant Giant Despair. They, therefore, I say, took with them the head of the Giant, for his body they had buried under a heap of stones, and down to the road and to their companions they came, and showed them what they had done.

Now I saw in my dream, when all these things were finished, Mr. Great-heart took the head of Giant Despair, and set it upon a pole by the highway side, right over against the pillar that Christian erected for a caution to pilgrims that came after, to take heed entering into his grounds.

> Though Doubting Castle be demolish'd,
> And the Giant Despair hath lost his head,
> Sin can rebuild the Castle, make't remain,
> And make Despair the Giant live again.

Then he writ under it, upon a marble stone, these verses following:

> This the head of him, whose name only
> In former times did pilgrims terrify.
> His Castle's down; and Diffidence, his wife,
> Brave Master Great-heart has bereft of life.
> Dispondency, his daughter Much-afraid,
> Great-heart for them also the man has play'd;
> Who hereof doubts, if he'll but cast his eye
> Up hither, may his scruples satisfy.
> This head also, when doubting cripples dance,
> Doth show from fears they have deliverance.

When these men had thus bravely showed themselves against Doubting Castle, and had slain Giant Despair, they went forward; and went on till they came to the Delectable Mountains, where Christian and Hopeful refreshed themselves with the varieties of the place. They also acquainted themselves with the shepherds there, who welcomed them, as they had done Christian before, unto the Delectable Mountains.

Now the Shepherds, seeing so great a train follow Mr. Great-heart, for with him they were well acquainted, they said unto him, Good Sir, you have got a goodly company here. Pray, where did you find all these?

Then Mr. Great-heart replied:

> First, here is Christiana, and her train,
> Her sons, and her sons' wives, who like the wain,
> Keep by the pole, and do by compass steer,
> From sin to grace, else they had not been here;
> Next, here's old Honest come on pilgrimage,
> Ready-to-halt, too, who, I dare engage,
> True-hearted is, and so is Feeble-mind,
> Who willing was not to be left behind;
> Dispondency, good man, is coming after,
> And so also is Much-afraid his daughter.
> May we have entertainment here, or must
> We farther go? Let's know whereon to trust.

Then said the Shepherds, This is a comfortable company. You are welcome to us, for we have comfort for the feeble as for the strong. Our Prince has an eye to what is done to the least of these; therefore infirmity must not be a block to our entertainment. So they had them to the palace door, and then said unto them, Come in, Mr. Feeble-mind; come in, Mr. Ready-to-halt; Come in, Mr. Dispondency, and Mrs. Much-afraid, his daughter. These, Mr. Great-heart, said the Shepherds to the guide, we call in by name, for that they are most subject to draw back; but as for you, and the rest that are strong, we leave you to your wonted liberty. Then said Mr. Great-heart, This day I see that grace doth shine in your faces, and that you are my Lord's Shepherds indeed; for that you have not pushed these diseased neither with side nor shoulder, but have rather strewed their way into the palace with flowers, as you should.

So the feeble and weak went in, and Mr. Great-heart and the rest did follow. When they were also set down, the Shepherds said to those of the weaker sort, What is it that you would have? for, said they, all things must be managed here to the supporting of the weak, as well as the warning of the unruly.

So they made them a feast of things easy of digestion, and that were pleasant to the palate, and nourishing; the which, when they had received, they went to their rest, each one respectively unto his proper place. When morning was come, because the mountains were high, and the day clear, and because it was the custom of the Shepherds to show to the Pilgrims, before their departure, some rarities; therefore, after they were ready, and had refreshed themselves, the Shepherds took them out into the fields, and showed them first what they showed to Christian before.

Then they had them to some new places. The first was to Mount Marvel, where they looked, and beheld a man at a distance, that tumbled the hills about with words. Then they asked the Shepherds what that sould mean? So they told them, that that man was a son of one Great-grace, of whom you read in the First Part of the Records of the Pilgrim's Progress. And he is set there to teach pilgrims how to believe down, or to tumble out of their way, what difficulties they shall meet with, by faith. Then said Mr. Great-heart, I know him. He is a man above many.

Then they had them to another place, called Mount Innocent; and there they saw a man cloathed all in white, and two men, Prejudice and Ill-will, continually casting dirt upon him. Now, behold, the dirt, whatsoever they cast at him, would in little time fall off again, and his garments would look as clear as if no dirt had been cast thereat.

Then said the Pilgrims, What means this? The Shepherds answered, This man is named Godly-man, and this garment is to show the innocency of his life. Now, those that throw dirt at him, are such as hate his well-doing; but, as you see the dirt will not stick upon his clothes, so it shall be with him that liveth truly innocently in the world. Whoever they be that would make such men dirty, they labour all in vain; for God, by that a little time is spent, will cause that their innocence shall break forth as the light, and their righteousness as the noon-day.

Then they took them, and had them to Mount Charity, where they showed them a man that had a bundle of cloth lying before him, out of which he cut coats and garments for the poor that stood about him; yet his bundle or roll of cloth was never the less.

Then said they, What should this be? This is, said the Shepherds, to show you, that he that has a heart to give of his labour to the poor, shall

112

never want wherewithal. He that watereth shall be watered himself. And the cake that the widow gave to the prophet did not cause that she had ever the less in her barrel.

They had them also to a place where they saw one Fool, and one Want-wit, washing of an Ethiopian, with intention to make him white; but the more they washed him the blacker he was. They then asked the Shepherds what that should mean. So they told them, saying, Thus shall it be with the vile person. All means used to get such a one a good name shall, in con-clusion, tend but to make him more abominable. Thus it was with the Pharisees, and so shall it be with all hypocrites.

Now when the Shepherds had shown them all these things, then they had them back to the place, and entertained them with what the house would afford. But Mercy being a young and breeding woman, longed for some-thing that she saw there, but was ashamed to ask. Her mother-in-law then asked her what she ailed; for she looked as one not well. Then said Mercy, There is a looking-glass hangs up in the dining-room, off which I cannot take my mind: if, therefore, I have it not, I think I shall miscarry. Then said her mother, I will mention thy wants to the Shepherds, and they will not deny it thee. But she said, I am ashamed that these men should know that I longed. Nay, my daughter, said she, it is no shame but a virtue, to long for such a thing as that. So Mercy said, Then, mother, if you please, ask the Shepherds if they are willing to sell it.

Now the glass was one of a thousand. It would present a man, one way, with his own features exactly; and, turn it but another way, and it would show one the very face and similitude of the Prince of Pilgrims himself. Yea, I have talked with them that can tell, and they have said, that they have seen the very crown of thorns upon his head, by looking in that glass; they have therein also seen the holes in his hands, in his feet, and his side. Yea, such an excellency is there in that glass, that it will show him to one where they have a mind to see him; whether living or dead; whether in earth or heaven; whether in a state of humiliation, or in his exaltation; whether coming to suffer, or coming to reign.

Christiana, therefore, went to the Shepherds apart—now the names of the Shepherds are Knowledge, Experience, Watchful, and Sincere—and said unto them, There is one of my daughters, a married woman, that I think doth long for something that she hath seen in this house; and she thinks she shall miscarry, if she shall by you be denied.

EXPERIENCE. Call her, call her; she shall assuredly have what can help her to. So they called her, and said to her, Mercy, what is that thing thou wouldst have? Then she blushed, and said, The great glass that hangs up in the dining-room. So Sincere ran and fetched it, and, with a joyful consent, it was given her. Then she bowed her head, and gave thanks, and said, By this I know that I have obtained favour in your eyes.

They also gave to the other young women such things as they desired, and to their husbands great commendations, for that they had joined with

Mr. Great-heart, to the slaying of Giant Despair, and the demolishing of Doubting Castle.

About Christiana's neck, the Shepherds put a bracelet, and so they did about the necks of her four daughters; also they put ear-rings in their ears, and jewels on their foreheads.

When they were minded to go hence, they let them go in peace, but gave not to them those certain cautions which before were given to Christian and his companion. The reason was, for that these had Great-heart to be their guide, who was one that was well acquainted with things, and so could give them their cautions more seasonably; to wit, even then when the danger was nigh the approaching.

What cautions Christian and his companion had received of the Shepherds, they had also lost, by that the time was come that they had need to put them in practice. Wherefore, here was the advantage that this company had over the other.

From hence they went on singing.

When they were gone from the Shepherds, they quickly came to the place where Christian met with one Turn-away, that dwelt in the town of Apostasy. Wherefore of him Mr. Great-heart, their guide, did now put them in mind, saying, This is the place where Christian met with one Turn-away, who carried with him the character of his rebellion at his back. And this I have to say concerning this man; he would hearken to no counsel, but once falling, persuasion could not stop him.

When he came to the place where the Cross and the Sepulchre were, he did meet with one that did bid him look there, but he gnashed with his teeth, and stamped, and said, he was resolved to go back to his own town. Before he came to the gate, he met with Evangelist, who offered to lay hands on him, to turn him into the way again. But this Turn-away resisted him, and having done much despite unto him, he got away over the wall, and so escaped his hand.

Then they went on; and just at the place where Little-faith formerly was robbed, there stood a man with his sword drawn, and his face all bloody. Then said Mr. Great-heart, What art thou? The man made answer, saying, I am one whose name is Valiant-for-truth. I am a pilgrim, and am going to the Celestial City. Now, as I was in my way, there were three men did beset me, and propounded unto me these three things: 1. Whether I would become one of them. 2. Or go back from whence I came. 3. Or die upon the place. To the first, I answered, I had been a true man a long season, and therefore it could not be expected that I now should cast in my lot with thieves. Then they demanded what I would say to the second. So I told them that the place from whence I came, had I not found incommodity there, I had not forsaken it at all; but finding it altogether unsuitable to me, and very unprofitable for me, I forsook it for this way. Then they asked me what I said to the third. And I told them, My life cost more dear far, than that I should lightly give it away. Besides, you have nothing to do thus to put things to my choice; wherefore, at your peril be it, if you meddle. Then these three, to wit, Wild-head, Inconsiderate, and Pragmatick, drew upon me, and I also drew upon them.

So we fell to it, one against three, for the space of above three hours. They have left upon me, as you see, some of the marks of their valour, and have also carried away with them some of mine. They are but just now gone. I suppose they might, as the saying is, hear your horse dash, and so they betook them to flight.

GREAT-HEART. But here was great odds, three against one.

VALIANT-FOR-TRUTH. It is true; but little or more are nothing to him that has the truth on his side. Though an host should encamp against me, said one, my heart shall not fear; though war should rise against me, in this will I be confident. Besides, saith he, I have read in some records, that one man has fought an army. And how many did Samson slay with the jaw-bone of an ass?

GREAT-HEART. Then said the guide, Why did you not cry out, that some might have come in for your succour?

VALIANT-FOR-TRUTH. So I did, to my King, who, I knew, could hear, and afford invisible help, and that was sufficient for me.

GREAT-HEART. Then said Great-heart to Mr. Valiant-for-truth. Thou hast worthily behaved thyself. Let me see thy sword. So he showed it him. When he had taken it in his hand, and looked thereon a while, he said, Ha! it is a right Jerusalem blade.

VALIANT-FOR-TRUTH. It is so. Let a man have one of these blades, with a hand to wield it and skill to use it, and he may venture upon an angel with it. He need not fear its holding, if he can but tell how to lay on. Its edges will never blunt. It will cut flesh and bones, and soul and spirit, and all.

GREAT-HEART. But you fought a great while; I wonder you was not weary.

VALIANT-FOR-TRUTH. I fought till my sword did cleave to my hand; and when they were joined together, as if a sword grew out of my arm, and when the blood ran through my fingers, then I fought with most courage.

GREAT-HEART. Thou hast done well. Thou hast resisted unto blood, striving against sin. Thou shalt abide by us, come in and go out with us, for we are thy companions.

Then they took him, and washed his wounds, and gave him of what they had to refresh him; and so they went on together. Now, as they went on, because Mr. Great-heart was delighted in him, for he loved one greatly that he found to be a man of his hands, and because there were with his company them that were feeble and weak, therefore he questioned with him about many things; as, first, what countryman he was?

VALIANT-FOR-TRUTH. I am of Dark-land; for there I was born, and there my father and mother are still.

GREAT-HEART. Dark-land, said the guide; doth not that lie up on the same coast with the City of Destruction?

VALIANT-FOR-TRUTH. Yes, it doth. Now, that which caused me to come on pilgrimage was this; we had one Mr. Tell-true came into our parts, and

115

he told it about what Christian had done, that went from the City of Destruction; namely, how he had forsaken his wife and children, and had betaken himself to a pilgrim's life. It was also confidently reported, how he had killed a serpent that did come out to resist him in his journey, and how he got through to whither he intended. It was also told, what welcome he had at all his Lord's lodgings, especially when he came to the gates of the Celestial City; for there, said the man, he was received with sound of trumpet, by a company of Shining Ones. He told it also, how all the bells in the city did ring for joy at his reception, and what golden garments he was cloathed with, with many other things that now I shall forbear to relate. In a word, that man so told the story of Christian and his travels, that my heart fell into a burning haste to be gone after him; nor could father or mother stay me! So I got from them, and am come thus far on my way.

GREAT-HEART. You came in at the gate, did you not?

VALIANT-FOR-TRUTH. Yes, yes; for the same man also told us that all would be nothing, if we did not begin to enter this way at the gate.

GREAT-HEART. Look you, said the guide to Christiana, the pilgrimage of your husband, and what he has gotten thereby, is spread abroad far and near.

VALIANT-FOR-TRUTH. Why, is this Christian's wife?

GREAT-HEART. Yes, that it is, and these are also her four sons.

VALIANT-FOR-TRUTH. What! and going on pilgrimage too?

GREAT-HEART. Yes, verily; they are following after.

VALIANT-FOR-TRUTH. It glads me at heart. Good man! how joyful will he be when he shall see them that would not go with him, yet to enter after him in at the gates into the City!

GREAT-HEART. Without doubt it will be a comfort to him; for, next to the joy of seeing himself there, it will be a joy to meet there his wife and children.

VALIANT-FOR-TRUTH. But, now you are upon that, pray let me hear your opinion about it. Some make a question, Whether we shall know one another when we are there.

GREAT-HEART. Do they think they shall know themselves then, or that they shall rejoice to see themselves in that bliss? and if they think they shall know and do these, why not know others, and rejoice in their welfare also?

Again, since relations are our second self, though that state will be dissolved there; yet why may it not be rationally concluded, that we shall be more glad to see them there, than to see they are wanting?

VALIANT-FOR-TRUTH. Well, I perceive whereabouts you are as to this. Have you any more things to ask me about my beginning to come on pilgrimage?

GREAT-HEART. Yes. Was your father and mother willing that you should become a pilgrim?

VALIANT-FOR-TRUTH. O no! They used all means imaginable to persuade me to stay at home.

116

GREAT-HEART. What could they say against it?

VALIANT-FOR-TRUTH. They said it was an idle life; and if I myself were not inclined to sloth and laziness, I would never countenance a pilgrim's condition.

GREAT-HEART. And what did they say else?

VALIANT-FOR-TRUTH. Why, they told me that it was a dangerous way; yea, the most dangerous way in the world, said they, is that which the pilgrims go.

GREAT-HEART. Did they show wherein this way is so dangerous?

VALIANT-FOR-TRUTH. Yes; and that in many particulars.

GREAT-HEART. Name some of them.

VALIANT-FOR-TRUTH. They told me of the Slough of Dispond, where Christian was well nigh smothered. They told me that there were archers standing ready in Beelzebub Castle, to shoot them that should knock at the wicket-gate for entrance. They told me also of the wood, and dark mountains; of the Hill Difficulty; of the lions; and also of the three giants, Bloody-man, Maul, and Slay-good. They said, moreover, that there was a foul fiend haunted the Valley of Humiliation, and that Christian was by him almost bereft of life. Besides, said they, you must go over the Valley of the Shadow of Death, where the hobgoblins are; where the light is darkness; where the way is full of snares, pits, traps, and gins. They told me also of Giant Despair, of Doubting Castle, and of the ruin that the Pilgrims met with there. Further, they said I must go over the Inchanted Ground, which was dangerous. And that, after all this, I should find a river, over which I should find no bridge, and that that river did lie betwixt me and the Celestial Country.

GREAT-HEART. And was this all?

VALIANT-FOR-TRUTH. No. They also told me that this way was full of deceivers, and of persons that laid in wait there to turn good men out of the path.

GREAT-HEART. But how did they make that out?

VALIANT-FOR-TRUTH. They told me that Mr. Worldly Wiseman did there lie in wait to deceive. They also said, that there was Formality and Hypocrisy continually on the road. They said also that By-ends, Talkative, or Demas would go near to gather me up; that the Flatterer would catch me in his net; or that, with green-headed Ignorance, I would presume to go on to the gate, from whence he always was sent back to the hole that was in the side of the hill, and made to go the by-way to hell.

GREAT-HEART. I promise you this was enough to discourage; but did they make an end here?

VALIANT-FOR-TRUTH. No; stay. They told me also of many that had tried that way of old, and that had gone a great way therein, to see if they could find something of the glory there, that so many had so much talked of from time to time; and how they came back again, and befooled themselves for setting a foot out of doors in that path, to the satisfaction of all the country. And they named several that did so; as Obstinate and Pliable,

117

Mistrust and Timorous, Turn-away and old Atheist, with several more, who, they said, had some of them, gone far to see if they could find; but not one of them found so much advantage by going as amounted to the weight of a feather.

GREAT-HEART. And did none of these things discourage you?

VALIANT-FOR-TRUTH. No; they seemed but as so many nothings to me.

GREAT-HEART. How came that about?

VALIANT-FOR-TRUTH. Why, I still believed what Mr. Telltrue had said, and that carried me beyond them all.

GREAT-HEART. Then this was your victory, even your faith.

VALIANT-FOR-TRUTH. It was so. I believed, and therefore came out, got into the way, fought all that set themselves against me, and, by believing, am come to this place.

By this time they were got to the Inchanted Ground, where the air naturally tended to make one drowsy; and that place was all grown over with briars and thorns, excepting here and there, where was an Inchanted Arbour, upon which if a man sits, or in which, if a man sleeps, it is a question, say some, whether ever he shall rise or wake again in this world. Over this forest, therefore, they went, both one and the other, and Mr. Great-heart went before, for that he was the guide; and Mr. Valiant-for-truth, he came behind, being there a guard, for fear, lest peradventure some fiend, or dragon, or giant, or thief, should fall upon their rear, and so do mischief. They went on here, each man with his sword drawn in his hand, for they knew it was a dangerous place. Also they cheered up one another as well as they could; Feeble-mind, Mr. Great-heart commanded, should come up after him, and Mr. Dispondency was under the eye of Mr. Valiant.

Now they had not gone far, but a great mist and darkness fell upon them all, so that they could scarce, for a great while, see the one the other; wherefore they were forced, for some time, to feel for one another by words; for they walked not by sight.

But any one must think that here was but sorry going for the best of them all; but how much worse for the women and children, who both of feet and heart, were but tender. Yet so it was, that through the encouraging words of he that led in the front, and of him that brought them up behind, they made a pretty good shift to wag along.

The way also was here very wearisome, through dirt and slabbiness. Nor was there on all this ground so much as one inn, or victualling house, therein to refresh the feebler sort. Here, therefore, was grunting, and puffing, and sighing. While one tumbleth over a bush, another sticks fast in the dirt; and the children, some of them, lost their shoes in the mire. While one cries out, I am down; and another, Ho! where are you? and a third, The bushes have got such fast hold on me, I think I cannot get away from them.

Then they came at an arbour, warm, and promising much refreshing to the Pilgrims; for it was finely wrought above head, beautified with greens,

118

furnished with benches and settles. It also had in it a soft couch, whereon they weary might lean. This, you must think, all things considered, was tempting; for the Pilgrims already began to be foiled with the badness of the way; but there was not one of them that made so much as a motion to stop there. Yea, for aught I could perceive, they continually gave so good heed to the advice of their guide, and he did so faithfully tell them of dangers, and of the nature of dangers, when they were at them, that usually, when they were nearest to them, they did most pluck up their spirits, and hearten one another to deny the flesh. This arbour was called The Slothful's Friend, on purpose to allure, if it might be, some of the pilgrims there to take up their rest when weary.

I saw then in my dream, that they went on in this their solitary ground, till they came to a place at which a man is apt to lose his way. Now, though when it was light, their guide could well enough tell how to miss those ways that led wrong, yet in the dark he was put to a stand; but he had in his pocket a map of all ways leading to, or from the Celestial City; wherefore he struck a light, for he never goes also without his tinder-box, and takes a view of his book or map, which bids him be careful, in that place, to turn to the right-hand way. And had he not here been careful to look in his map, they had all, in probability, been smothered in the mud; for, just a little before them, and that at the end of the cleanest way too, was a pit none knows how deep, full of nothing but mud, there made on purpose to destroy the Pilgrims in.

Then thought I with myself, who that goeth on pilgrimage, but would have one of these maps about him, that he may look when he is at a stand, which is the way he must take.

They went on, then, in this Inchanted Ground, till they came to where there was another arbour, and it was built by the highway-side. And in that arbour there lay two men, whose names were Heedless and Too-bold. These two went thus far on pilgrimage; but here, being wearied with their journey, they sat down to rest themselves, and so fell fast asleep. When the Pilgrims saw them, they stood still, and shook their heads; for they knew that the sleepers were in a pitiful case. Then they consulted what to do, whether to go on and leave them in their sleep, or to step to them, and try to awake them. So they concluded to go to them, and awake them; that is, if they could; but with this caution, namely, to take heed that themselves did not sit down nor embrace the offered benefit of that arbour.

So they went in, and spake to the men, and called each by his name, for the guide, it seems, did know them; but there was no voice nor answer. Then the guide did shake them, and do what he could to disturb them. Then said one of them, I will pay you when I take my money. At which the guide shook his head. I will fight so long as I can hold my sword in my hand, said the other. At that one of the children laughed.

Then said Christiana, What is the meaning of this? The guide said, They talk in their sleep. If you strike them, beat them, or whatever you do to them, they will answer you after this fashion; or, as one of them said in old time, when the waves of the sea did beat upon him, and he slept as one upon the mast of a ship, When shall I awake? I will seek it yet again. You know, when men talk in their sleep, they say anything, but their words are not governed either by faith or reason. There is an incoherency in their words now, as there was before, betwixt their going on pilgrimage, and sitting down here. This, then, is the mischief of it, when heedless ones go on pilgrimage, it is twenty to one but they are served thus; for this Inchanted Ground is one of the last refuges that the enemy to pilgrims has. Wherefore it is, as you see, placed almost at the end of the way, and so it standeth against us with the more advantage. For when, thinks the enemy, will these fools be so desirous to sit down, as when they are weary? and when so like to be weary, as when almost at their journey's end? Therefore it is, I say, that the Inchanted Ground is placed so nigh to the Land Beulah, and so near the end of their race. Wherefore, let pilgrims look to themselves, lest it happen to them as it has done to these, that, as you see, are fallen asleep, and none can wake them.

Then the Pilgrims desired, with trembling, to go forward; only they prayed their guide to strike a light, that they might go the rest of their way by the help of the light of a lantern. So he struck a light, and they went by the help of that through the rest of this way, though the darkness was very great.

But the children began to be sorely weary; and they cried out unto him that loveth pilgrims, to make their way more comfortable. So by that they had gone a little further, a wind arose, that drove away the fog; so the air became more clear.

Yet they were not off, by much, of the Inchanted Ground, only now they could see one another better, and the way wherein they should walk.

Now, when they were almost at the end of this ground, they perceived that, a little way before them, was a solemn noise as of one that was much concerned. So they went on and looked before them; and behold, they saw, as they thought, a man upon his knees, with hands and eyes lift up, and speaking as they thought, earnestly to one that was above. They drew nigh, but could not tell what he said. So they went softly till he had done. When he had done, he got up, and began to run towards the Celestial City. Then Mr. Great-heart called after him, saying, Soho! friend, let us have your company, if you go, as I suppose you do, to the Celestial City. So the man stopped, and they came up to him. But so soon as Mr. Honest saw him, he said, I know this man. Then said Mr. Valiant-for-truth, Prithee, who is it? It is one, said he, who comes from whereabouts I dwelt. His name is Stand-fast; he is certainly a right good pilgrim.

So they came up one to another; and presently Stand-fast said to old Honest, Ho, father Honest, are you there? Aye, said he, that I am, as sure as you are there. Right glad am I, said Mr. Stand-fast, that I have found you on this road. And as glad am I, said the other, that I espied you upon your knees. Then Mr. Stand-fast blushed, and said, But why, did you see me? Yes, that I did, quoth the other, and with my heart was glad at the

120

sight. Why, what did you think? said Stand-fast. Think! said old Honest, what should I think? I thought we had an honest man upon the road, and therefore should have his company by and by. If you thought not amiss (said Standfast), how happy am I; but if I be not as I should, I alone must bear it. That is true, said the other; but your fear doth further confirm me, that things are right betwixt the Prince of Pilgrims and your soul; for, saith he, Blessed is the man that feareth always.

VALIANT-FOR-TRUTH. Well, but brother, I pray thee tell us what was it that was the cause of thy being upon thy knees even now? Was it for that some special mercies laid obligations upon thee, or how?

STAND-FAST. Why, we are, as you see, upon the Inchanted Ground; and as I was coming along, I was musing with myself of what a dangerous road the road in this place was, and how many that had come even thus far on pilgrimage had here been stopped, and been destroyed. I thought also of the manner of the death with which this place destroyeth men. Those that die here, die of no violent distemper, The death which such die is not grievous to them; for he that goeth away in a sleep, begins that journey with desire and pleasure; yea, such acquiesce in the will of that disease.

HONEST. Then Mr. Honest, interrupting of him, said, Did you see the two men asleep in the arbour?

STAND-FAST. Aye, aye, I saw Heedless and Too-bold there; and, for aught I know, there they will lie till they rot. But let me go in my tale. As I was thus musing, as I said, there was one, in very pleasant attire, but old, who presented herself unto me, and offered me two things; to wit, her purse, and her bed. Now, the truth is, I was both a-weary and sleepy; I am also as poor as an owlet, and that, perhaps, the witch knew. Well, I repulsed her once and twice, but she put by my repulses, and smiled. Then I began to angry; but she mattered that nothing at all. Then she made offers again, and said, If I would be ruled by her, she would make me great and happy; for, said she, I am the mistress of the world, and men are made happy by me. Then I asked her name, and she told me it was Madam Bubble. This set me farther from her; but she still followed me with enticements. Then I betook me as you saw, to my knees; and with hands lift up, and cries, I prayed to him that had said he would help. So, just as you came up, the gentlewoman went her way. Then I continued to give thanks for this my great deliverance; for I verily believe she intended no good, but rather sought to make stop of me in my journey.

HONEST. Without doubt her designs were bad. But stay, now you talk of her, methinks I either have seen her, or have read some story of her.

STAND-FAST. Perhaps you have done both.

HONEST. Madam Bubble! is she not a tall, comely dame, something of a swarthy complexion?

STAND-FAST. Right, you hit it, she is just such a one.

HONEST. Doth she not speak very smoothly, and give you a smile at the end of a sentence?

STAND-FAST. You fall right upon it again, for these are her very actions.

HONEST. Doth she not wear a great purse by her side; and is not her hand often in it, fingering her money, as if that was her heart's delight.

STAND-FAST. It is just so; had she stood by all this while, you could not more amply have set her forth before me, nor have better described her features.

HONEST. Then he that drew her picture was a good limner, and he that wrote of her said true.

GREAT-HEART. This woman is a witch, and it is by virtue of her sorceries, that this ground is inchanted. Whoever doth lay their head down in her lap, had as good lay it down upon that block over which the axe doth hang; and whoever lay their eyes upon her beauty, are counted the enemies of God. This is she that maintaineth in their splendour all those that are the enemies of pilgrims. Yea, this is she that hath bought off many a man from a pilgrim's life. She is a great gossiper; she is always, both she and her daughters, at one pilgrim's heels or another, now commending, and then preferring the excellencies of this life. She is a bold and impudent slut; she will talk with any man. She always laugheth poor pilgrims to scorn; but highly commends the rich. If there be one cunning to get money in a place, she will speak well of him from house to house; she loveth banqueting and feasting mainly well; she is always at one full table or another. She has given it out in some places, that she is a goddess, and therefore some do worship her. She has her times and open places of cheating; and she will say and avow it, that none can show a good comparable to hers. She promiseth to dwell with children's children, if they will but love and make much of her. She will cast out of her purse gold like dust, in some places, and to some persons. She loves to be sought after, spoken well of, and to lie in the bosoms of men. She is never weary of commending her commodities, and she loves them most that think best of her. She will promise to some crowns and kingdoms, if they will but take her advice; yet many hath she brought to the halter, and ten thousand times more to hell.

STAND-FAST. O, said Stand-fast, what a mercy is it that I did resist! for whither might she have drawn me!

GREAT-HEART. Whither! nay, none but God knows whither. But, in general, to be sure, she would have drawn thee into many foolish and hurtful lusts, which drown men in destruction and perdition.

It was she that set Absalom against his father, and Jeroboam against his master. It was she that persuaded Judas to sell his Lord, and that prevailed with Demas to forsake the godly pilgrims' life; none can tell of the mischief that she doth. She makes variance betwixt rulers and subjects, betwixt parents and children, betwixt neighbour and neighbour, betwixt a man and his wife, betwixt a man and himself, betwixt the flesh and the heart.

Wherefore, good Master Stand-fast, be as your name is, and when you have done all, Stand.

At this discourse there was, among the Pilgrims, a mixture of joy and trembling.

122

After this, I beheld until they were come unto the Land of Beulah, where the sun shineth night and day. Here, because they were weary, they betook themselves a while to rest; and, because this country was common for pilgrims, and because the orchards and vineyards that were here belonged to the King of the Celestial Country, therefore they were licensed to make bold with any of his things. But a little while soon refreshed them here; for the bells did so ring, and the trumpets continually sound so melodiously, that they could not sleep; and yet they received as much refreshing, as if they had slept their sleep ever so soundly. Here also all the noise of them that walked in the streets, was, More pilgrims are come to town. And another would answer, saying, And so many went over the water, and were let in at the golden gates today. They would cry again, There is now a legion of Shining Ones, just come to town, by which we know that there are more pilgrims upon the road; for here they come to wait for them, and to comfort them after all their sorrow. Then the Pilgrims got up, and walked to and fro; but how were their ears now filled with heavenly noises, and their eyes delighted with celestial visions! In this land they heard nothing, saw nothing, felt nothing, smelled nothing, tasted nothing, that was offensive to their stomach or mind; only when they tasted of the water of the river over which they were to go, they thought that tasted a little bitterish to the palate, but it proved sweeter when it was down.

In this place there was a record kept of the names of them that had been pilgrims of old, and a history of all the famous acts that they had done. It was here also much discoursed how the river to some had had its flowings, and what ebbings it has had while others have gone over. It has been in a manner dry for some, while it has overflowed its banks for others.

In this place the children of the town would go into the King's gardens, and gather nosegays for the Pilgrims, and bring them to them with much affection. Here also grew camphire, with spikenard, and saffron, calamus, and cinnamon, with all its trees of frankincense, myrrh, and aloes, with all chief spices. With these the Pilgrims' chambers were perfumed, while they staid here; and with these were their bodies anointed, to prepare them to go over the river when the time appointed was come.

Now, while they lay here, and waited for the good hour, there was a noise in the town, that there was a post come from the Celestial City, with matter of great importance to one Christiana, the wife of Christian the Pilgrim. So enquiry was made for her, and the house was found out where she was; so the post presented her with a letter; the contents whereof were, Hail, good woman! I bring thee tidings that the Master calleth for thee, and expecteth that thou shouldest stand in his presence, in clothes of immortality, within these ten days.

When he had read this letter to her, he gave her therewith a sure token that he was a true messenger, and was come to bid her make haste to be gone. The token was, an arrow with a point sharpened with love, let easily into her heart, which by degrees wrought so effectually with her, that at the time appointed she must be gone.

When Christiana saw that her time was come, and that she was the first of this company that was to go over, she called for Mr. Great-heart her guide, and told him how matters were. So he told her he was heartily glad of the news, and could have been glad had the post come for him. Then she bid that he should give advice how all things should be prepared for her journey. So he told her, saying, thus and thus it must be; and we that survive will accompany you to the river side.

Then she called for her children, and gave them her blessing, and told them, that she yet read with comfort the mark that was set in their foreheads, and was glad to see them with her there, and that they had kept their garments so white. Lastly, she bequeathed to the poor that little she had, and commanded her sons and her daughters to be ready against the messenger should come for them.

When she had spoken these words to her guide and to her children, she called for Mr. Valiant-for-truth, and said unto him, Sir, you have in all places showed yourself true-hearted; be faithful unto death, and my King will give you a crown of life. I would also entreat you to have an eye to my children; and if at any time you see them faint, speak comfortably to them. For my daughters, my sons' wives, they have been faithful, and a fulfilling of the promise upon them will be their end. But she gave Mr. Stand-fast a ring.

Then she called for old Mr. Honest, and said of him, Behold an Israelite indeed, in whom is no guile. Then said he, I wish you a fair day, when you set out for Mount Zion, and shall be glad to see that you go over the river dry-shod. But she answered, Come wet, come dry, I long to be gone; for, however the weather is in my journey, I shall have time enough when I come there to sit down and rest me, and dry me.

Then came in that good man Mr. Ready-to-halt, to see her. So she said to him, Thy travel hither has been with difficulty; but that will make thy rest the sweeter. But watch and be ready; for at an hour when you think not, the messenger may come.

After him came in Mr. Dispondency, and his daughter Much-afraid, to whom she said, You ought with thankfulness, for ever to remember your deliverance from the hands of Giant Despair, and out of Doubting Castle. The effect of that mercy is, that you are brought with safety hither. Be ye watchful, and cast away fear; be sober and hope to the end.

Then she said to Mr. Feeble-mind, Thou wast delivered from the mouth of Giant Slay-good, that thou mightest live in the light of the living for ever, and see thy King with comfort; only I advise thee to repent thee of thine aptness to fear and doubt of his goodness, before he sends for thee; lest thou shouldest, when he comes, be forced to stand before him, for that fault, with blushing.

Now the day drew on, that Christiana must be gone. So the road was full of people to see her take her journey. But, behold, all the banks beyond the river were full of horses and chariots, which were come down from above to accompany her to the city gate. So she came forth, and entered the river, with a beckon of farewell to those that followed her to the river side. The last words that she was heard to say here, were, I come, Lord, to be with thee, and bless thee.

So her children and friends returned to their place, for that those that waited for Christiana had carried her out of their sight. So she went and called, and entered in at the gate with all the ceremonies of joy that her husband Christian had done before her.

At her departure her children wept. But Mr. Great-heart and Mr. Valiant played upon the well-tuned cymbal and harp for joy. So all departed to their respective places.

In process of time there came a post to the town again, and his business was with Mr. Ready-to-halt. So he enquired him out, and said to him, I am come to thee in the name of him whom thou hast loved and followed, though upon crutches; and my message is to tell thee, that he expects thee at his table to sup with him, in his kingdom, the next day after Easter; wherefore prepare thyself for this journey.

Then he also gave him a token that he was a true messenger, saying, I have broken thy golden bowl,and loosed thy silver cord.

After this, Mr. Ready-to-halt called for his fellow-pilgrims, and told them, saying, I am sent for, and God shall surely visit you also. So he desired Mr. Valiant to make his will; and because he had nothing to bequeath to them that should survive him, but his crutches, and his good wishes, therefore thus he said, These crutches I bequeath to my son that shall tread in my steps, with a hundred warm wishes that he may prove better than I have done.

Then he thanked Mr. Great-heart for his conduct and kindness, and so addressed himself to his journey. When he came at the brink of the river, he said, Now I shall have no more need of these crutches, since yonder are chariots and horses for me to ride on. The last words he was heard to say was, Welcome life! So he went his way.

After this Mr. Feeble-mind had tidings brought him, that the post sounded his horn at his chamber door. Then he came in, and told him, saying, I am come to tell thee, that thy Master hath need of thee; and that, in very little time, thou must behold his face in brightness. And take this as a token of the truth of my message, Those that look out of the windows shall be darkened.

Then Mr. Feeble-mind called for his friends, and told them what errand had been brought unto him, and what token he had received of the truth of the message. Then he said, Since I have nothing to bequeath to any, to what purpose should I make a will? As for my feeble mind, that I will leave behind me, for that I have no need of that in the place whither I go. Nor is it worth bestowing upon the poorest pilgrim; wherefore, when I am gone, I desire that you, Mr. Valiant, would bury it in a dung-hill. This done, and the day being come in which he was to depart, he entered the river as the rest. His last words were, Hold out, faith and patience. So he went over to the other side.

125

When days had many of them passed away, Mr. Dispondency was sent for; for a post was come, and brought this message to him: Trembling man, these are to summon thee to be ready with thy King by the next Lord's day, to shout for joy for thy deliverance from all thy doubtings.

And, said the messenger, that my message is true, take this for a proof; so he gave him the grasshopper to be a burden unto him. Now, Mr. Dispondency's daughter, whose name was Much-afraid, said, when she heard what was done, that she would go with her father. Then Mr. Dispondency said to his friends, Myself and my daughter, you know what we have been, and how troublesomely we have behaved ourselves in every company. My will and my daughter's is, that our desponds and slavish fears be by no man ever received, from the day of our departure, for ever; for I know that after my death they will offer themselves to others. For, to be plain with you, they are ghosts the which we entertained when we first began to be pilgrims, and could never shake them off after; and they will walk about and seek entertainment of the pilgrims; but, for our sakes, shut ye the doors upon them.

When the time was come for them to depart, they went to the brink of the river. The last words of Mr. Dispondency were, Farewell night, welcome day. His daughter went through the river singing, but none could understand what she said.

Then it came to pass, a while after, that there was a post in the town that enquired for Mr. Honest. So he came to his house where he was, and delivered to his hand these lines: Thou art commanded to be ready against this day sevennight, to present thyself before thy Lord, at his Father's house. And for a token that my message is true, All thy daughters of musick shall be brought low. Then Mr. Honest called for his friends, and said unto them, I die, but shall make no will. As for my honesty, it shall go with me; let him that comes after be told of this. When the day that he was to be gone was come, he addressed himself to go over the river. Now the river at that time overflowed the banks in some places; but Mr. Honest in his lifetime had spoken to one Good-conscience to meet him there, the which he also did, and lent him his hand, and so helped him over. The last words of Mr. Honest were, Grace reigns. So he left the world.

After this, it was noised abroad, that Mr. Valiant-for-truth was taken with a summons, by the same post as the other; and had this for a token that the summons was true, That his pitcher was broken at the fountain. When he understood it, he called for his friends, and told them of it. Then, said he, I am going to my Father's; and though with great difficulty I am got hither, yet now I do not repent me of all the trouble I have been at to arrive where I am. My sword I give to him that shall succeed me in my pilgrimage, and my courage and skill to him that can get it. My marks and scars I carry with me, to be a witness for me, that I have fought his battles, who now will be my rewarder. When the day that he must go hence was come, many accompanied him to the river side, into which as he went, he said, Death, where is thy sting? And as he went down deeper, he said,

Grave, where is thy victory? So he passed over, and all the trumpets sounded for him on the other side.

Then there came forth a summons for Mr. Stand-fast—this Mr. Standfast he that the rest of the Pilgrims found upon his knees in the Inchanted Ground—for the post brought it him open in his hands. The contents whereof were, that he must prepare for a change of life, for his Master was not willing that he should be so far from him any longer. At this Mr. Standfast was put into a muse. Nay, said the messenger, you need not doubt of the truth of my message, for here is a token of the truth thereof: Thy wheel is broken at the cistern. Then he called unto him Mr. Great-heart, who was their guide, and said unto him, Sir, although it was not my hap to be much in your good company in the days of my pilgrimage; yet, since the time I knew you, you have been profitable to me. When I came from home, I left behind me a wife and five small children; let me entreat you, at your return (for I know that you will go, and return to your Master's house, in hopes that you may yet be a conductor to more of the holy pilgrims), that you send to my family, and let them be acquainted with all that hath, or shall happen unto me. Tell them, moreover, of my happy arrival to this place, and of the present [and] late blessed condition that I am in. Tell them also of Christian, and Christiana his wife, and how she and her children came after her husband. Tell them also of what a happy end she made, and whither she is gone. I have little or nothing to send to my family, except it be prayers and tears for them; of which it will suffice if thou acquaint them, if peradventure they may prevail.

When Mr. Stand-fast had thus set things in order, and the time being come for him to haste him away, he also went down to the river. Now there was a great calm at that time in the river; wherefore Mr. Stand-fast, when he was about halfway in, stood a while and talked to his companions that had waited upon him thither; and he said, This river has been a terror to many; yea, the thoughts of it also have often frightened me. But now, methinks, I stand easy, my foot is fixed upon that upon which the feet of the priests that bare the ark of the covenant stood, while Israel went over this Jordan. The waters, indeed, are to the palate bitter, and to the stomach cold; yet the thoughts of what I am going to, and of the conduct that waits for me on the other side, doth lie as a glowing coal at my heart.

I see myself now at the end of my journey, my toilsome days are ended. I am going now to see that head that was crowned with thorns, and that face was spit upon for me.

I have formerly lived by hearsay and faith; but now I go where I shall live by sight, and shall be with him in whose company I delight myself.

I have loved to hear my Lord spoken of; and wherever I have seen the print of his shoe in the earth, there I have coveted to set my foot too.

His name has been to me as a civet-box; yea, sweeter than all perfumes. His voice to me has been most sweet; and his countenance I have more desired than they that have most desired the light of the sun. His word I did use to gather for my food, and for antidotes against my faintings. He has held me, and hath kept me from mine iniquities; yea, my steps hath he strengthened in his way.

Now, while he was thus in discourse, his countenance changed, his strong man bowed under him; and after he had said, Take me, for I come unto thee, he ceased to be seen of them.

But glorious it was to see how the open region was filled with horses and chariots, with trumpeters and pipers, with singers and players on stringed instruments, to welcome the Pilgrims as they went up, and followed one another in at the beautiful gate of the city.

As for Christian's children, the four boys that Christiana brought with her, with their wives and children, I did not stay where I was till they were gone over. Also, since I came away, I heard one say that they were yet alive, and so would be for the increase of the church in that place where they were, for a time.

Shall it be my lot to go that way again, I may give those that desire it an account of what I here am silent about. Meantime, I bid my reader

ADIEU

THE CONCLUSION

Now, Reader, I have told my dream to thee;
See if thou canst interpret it to me,
Or to thyself, or neighbour; but take heed
Of misinterpreting; for that, instead
Of doing good, will but thyself abuse:
By misinterpreting, evil ensues.

Take heed also, that thou be not extreme,
In playing with the outside of my dream:
Nor let my figure or similitude
Put thee into a laughter or a feud.
Leave this for boys and fools; but as for thee,
Do thou the substance of my matter see.

Put by the curtains, look within my veil,
Turn up my metaphors, and do not fail;
There, if thou seekest them, such things to find,
As will be helpful to an honest mind.

What of my dross thou findest there, be bold
To throw away, but yet preserve the gold;
What if my gold be wrapped up in ore?—
None throws away the apple for the core.
But if thou shalt cast all sin away as vain,
I know not but 'twill make me dream again.

Printed in Germany